A Stranger in Burkeville

David Osborne

WILLIAMS & COMPANY
BOOK PUBLISHERS

Books by David Osborne

An Appalachian Childhood

Manufactured in the United States of America

A Jake Harn Novel

ISBN 978-1-878853-92-9

This book is dedicated to all my brothers and sisters, who had the imagination to play cowboys and Indians with me. It is also dedicated to all the young buckaroos who spent hour after hour replaying the western mystique and to all the old galoots like me who remember those days.

One

Willow Springs, Kansas consisted of two buildings: a small lean-to that could shelter a couple of horses and a larger building that housed a trading post on the first floor and living quarters on the second. Attached to the lean-to was a small corral that could hold a half a dozen horses.

Jake Harn had smelled smoke before he was in sight of the building.

In this desolate country, any signs of civilization were far and few between, so when the opportunity came along Jake was always willing to stop over. He reined in his horse, looked up at the sun and gauged the time to be a little after noon. He took off his hat and mopped his brow with his shirt sleeve. He knocked the trail dust off his shirt and pants with his hat and looked back at the settlement. After a few moments he put his hat back on his head and nudged his horse toward the two buildings.

As he rode closer he noticed a small spring flowing off a small rock-covered bank. The water trickled down to the bottom creating a small pool that held enough water for a few people or animals. The original spring had been very small, Jake surmised, but someone had enlarged it to its present width and depth.

Jake stepped down, allowing his horse to take a drink from the spring and then tied him at a rickety rail held up by two time and wind-worn posts in front of the trading post. Three horses and a donkey were tied to the rail, the horses still saddled and lazily swatting flies with their tails. The donkey held a load that was hidden by a canvas cover, but Jake could tell that it had just been ridden. The animal had sensed the nearby water and was trying to get to the spring. Jake untied the donkey and led him to water. After the animal drank his fill, Jake tied him back at the same rail.

Jake filled up his canteens from the spring and hung them on his saddle horn. He slipped his rifle from the scabbard and glanced around again. Nothing caught his eye as he stepped up on the porch and opened the door to the trading post. His first look revealed a fairly large room. Make-shift shelves held flour, coffee, salt and other supplies necessary for the few travelers that would happen by. Next to the food items were a few guns, ammunition and leather goods needed to mend saddles or bridles. It was not a large supply, but it would last a man until he could get to a larger town.

On one side of the room were some boards, supported by upturned whiskey barrels, creating a temporary bar. Behind it were several shelves laden with alcohol but few glasses. There were no tables for the patrons to use, assuming that there would ever be enough of them to need one.

The man behind the bar had a scraggly beard and a gut that burst freely over his belt. He didn't appear to be very steady on his feet, and Jake surmised that by his actions he had been sampling his own merchandise.

Jake shifted his glance toward the patrons and saw what appeared to be three ordinary cowboys. His gaze then moved to a fourth person, a strange little man in a black frockcoat and wearing a stovepipe hat. His appearance held Jake's attention for a minute. He was short and squat with wire-rimmed glasses. The little man was apparently giving a speech, but he was having a hard time getting the cowboys to listen. When Jake moved closer he heard the little man's obvious easterner voice saying, "My name is Lattimore Q. Cranbrook and I represent the Colt Manufacturing Company of Connecticut."

"What is a Connicket?" asked one of the boisterous cowboys.

"You, sir, are obviously uncouth and without proper education and manners," said the easterner, as if he were speaking to a child. "Connecticut is one of the first states in this Republic."

The cowboy moved closer and answered the little man saying, "Why don't you just teach us some of those proper manners that you're talking about?"

The little man sensed that he might have stepped over his bounds and he took a step backwards. "Mister, I …" he began quickly, en route to an apology.

But one of the other cowboys pushed him from behind. "Mister, we make our own manners and we don't need no dude in fancy britches to preach to us."

The first cowboy grabbed the hat from the easterner's head and stuffed it on his own head with more force than necessary.

"Watch out for the hat," Mr. Cranbrook demanded. "That hat cost me more than all of the clothes that you own."

"In this part of the country hats are not considered proper unless they have at least one hole in them. Putting some holes in it will increase the value," said the cowboy with the hat. He threw the hat in the air and the second cowboy drew his gun and quickly shot two holes in the hat. The first cowboy then picked the hat off the floor and said, "Let's just see how many holes we can put in this hat before it touches the ground."

The little man lunged for the hat but the cowboy simply shoved him away, causing the little man to bounce off the temporary bar and fall to the floor. The cowboy with the hat laughed at the little man and drew his gun. But before he could shoot, Jake moved toward the bar, intentionally jostling him.

The cowboy turned toward Jake.

"Who the hell are you?"

"Harn."

"Well, Harn, or whatever your name is, move out of the way!"

"Mister, I believe that this is a bar, and I am ordering a drink."

"This little man needs some learnin' and we are going to oblige, so I would suggest that you butt out."

"Mister, I am not concerned about your teaching, I just need enough room at the bar to get a drink," replied Jake.

The bartender, who obviously was enjoying the rough-housing of the little man, looked at Jake and snarled, "Git your drink somewhe'r else. These are my friends and they can do whatever they want."

Jake placed his rifle on the bar and said to the bartender, "Mighty unfriendly gents holed up here, Barkeep. I would love to drink somewhere else but this appears to be the only watering hole left, now get me a beer!"

The bartender moved up to the bar and faced Jake. "I decide who'll get a drink and I decide you don't git one." He started to turn away but Jake quickly reached over the makeshift bar, grabbed the greasy shirt of the bartender with his left hand and pulled him over the bar. With his right hand he grabbed the bartender behind his head and slammed his face against the bar. When Jake pulled the bartender's head up, blood oozed from his nose and a knot began forming on his forehead. "Now, how about that beer?" asked Jake.

The bartender didn't speak but looked at Jake with loathing. He glanced at the other three men for help and saw that none was coming. He stared at them and then looked back at Jake. After a moment's hesitation he walked down to the end of the bar and drew a beer. He set it on the bar in front of Jake with enough force to cause some of the contents to spill out.

Jake looked at the three men and spoke, "No offense to you but your bartender friend also needed some learning. I certainly hope that you don't mind."

The man that Jake bumped into at the bar glared into the cold eyes of Harn and decided that the fun was no longer important. He looked at the other two and they backed away. At this point Jake was sure that the bartender was on his own. Jake picked up the beer looked at the bartender and said, "Thank you kindly, Friend."

The bartender ignored Jake, walked down to the end of bar, and started to reach underneath.

"Friend, if you come up with a gun in your hand, you will be a dead man," cautioned Jake.

The bartender jerked straight up and looked at the other men and again saw no help coming. He picked up a dirty bar rag and started trying to wipe off the bar.

Jake picked up the mug and held it for a moment and then dumped it on the bar in front of him. "Here's to you and friendly service," he said as he glanced toward the bartender while tossing a coin in his direction. The bartender looked at Jake with pure hatred in his eyes but said nothing. Jake picked up his rifle, turned and walked out of the saloon.

He stepped off the porch and was just beginning to step into the saddle when the easterner came out of the door and hollered, "Wait, friend, I would like a word with you, if I may."

Jake looked him up and down and retorted, "Mister, I don't think that you or I have any friends in this place."

"Well, sir, I will not argue with that, but I would like to introduce myself. My name is Lattimore Q. Cranbrook and I ..."

Jake interrupted him and said, "I already know your name and that you are from Connecticut and the other gents didn't care and neither do I."

"But, Mister, if you would just permit me to ..."

Jake interrupted again and said, "Mr. Lattimore Q. Cranbrook – by the way, what does the 'Q' stand for?"

"Quincy, Sir. My Grandfather was a good friend of President John Quincy Adams."

"Quincy", Jake rolled it over his tongue and then said, "Well, Mr. Lattimore Quincy Cranbrook, I have some riding to do, so good luck to you."

Jake placed the rifle in the scabbard and stepped in the saddle. He glanced at the door of the trading post, spurred his horse and rode away. After a few hundred yards he looked back and saw the easterner charging after him riding the donkey. Jake turned and rode on, but soon Lattimore drew along side, close enough that Jake could have reached out and pushed him off the donkey.

Jake looked down at him and the little man said, "How about me just riding along with you for awhile?"

"Where are you going?" asked Jake without a hint of friendliness.

"Well, sir, I am not sure, but I am surely looking for civilization."

"In this country, civilization could be a long way away." Jake looked at the little man and decided that even though he was a pompous ass it would not hurt for him to ride along for awhile. "Okay, you can ride along," said Jake, "but we are going to have to settle this name issue."

The little man started to protest but Jake interrupted him and said, "I am not spending my time saying Lattimore Quincy Cranbrook. Now, if you have any friends, what do they call you?"

"Well, my Mother called me Quincy, bless her heart."

"As much as I hate it, I'll call you Quincy."

"Thank you, Sir; you will not regret your decision."

Jake looked over at the little man and his loaded donkey and muttered, "Wanna bet?"

Quincy looked at Jake and asked, "What did you say?"

"Oh nothing, I was just muttering to my horse."

The two rode for some time in silence and the little man asked, "It is awful hot and dry around here, is it possible that we could find some water?"

"Not much water around here, you have to carry it with you. Do you have a canteen?"

"No, Sir, I am not in the habit of carrying water with me."

"Well, Quincy, I would suggest that you get in the habit if you want to survive in this country," replied Jake.

He turned around and took an extra canteen off his saddle and pitched it to Quincy who said nothing but quickly took off the lid and drank deeply.

Jake looked at Quincy and said, "Water is very scarce in this territory and you need to fill up when you can. If we are lucky, we will find water and some shade on down the road. When we do we will make camp for the night."

"It won't be too soon for me," Quincy replied.

After a few yards of riding, Jake's horse startled a group of prairie hens. Just as they started to fly, Jake pulled out his pistol and knocked one of them out of the air. He rode the few feet over to it, dismounted, picked up the hen, and fastened it on the saddle.

As he came back, Quincy smiled and said, "Good

shooting, but why did you not shoot more? You had plenty of ammunition."

"The smart man shoots only what he needs and leaves the rest for the next person," explained Jake.

Quincy looked surprised, but Jake ignored him and rode on.

After a few hours the two men rode up to a small ravine with some shrub trees covering a waterhole. Jake pulled up his horse and motioned for his companion to do so. After surveying the layout for several minutes he spoke to Quincy, "This is as good a place as we can find. We will stop here for the night."

Quincy muttered and groaned as he dismounted his donkey. "I was beginning to think that we were going to ride all day and night."

Jake ignored the little man's complaining and said, "Get the saddle and pack off that donkey and get him some water."

"I'll just sit down for a moment and take care of that later."

Jake stared at the little man and said, "If you want this animal to get you to civilization, I would suggest that you take better care of him than you do yourself."

The little man begrudgingly unloaded the donkey and allowed him to drink. Jake took the reins of the donkey and his horse and led them to a small sapling. He tied them to the tree. He didn't worry about Muddy but he wanted to make sure that the donkey would not run off during the night.

He then went about gathering up enough wood to build a fire. When he was finished he addressed Quincy, "Do you have any food in that pack?"

"Of course not, this contains my wares," he replied.

"Quincy. What kinda' name is Quincy, anyway?" Before the little man could answer Jake said "Aw, never mind." He took the rifle out of the scabbard and leaned it against a small tree. In preparation of the meal he took the prairie hen off his saddle and emptied his saddle bags taking out a few beans, biscuits and coffee grounds, left-over from earlier in the morning.

Wood was scarce but Jake had found enough to build a small fire. When the fire was going he plucked the feathers from the hen and gutted it. He took two small pieces of wood and drove them into the ground. He found a longer piece, stuck it through the hen and laid the ends of the stick on the small upright pieces in the ground. The hen was close enough to the fire to cook, so he began fixing the rest of the meal.

Jake explored the area for more fire wood. He wanted enough to keep a small fire going during the night. When he got back to the camp he decided that the hen was done enough to eat. He beckoned Quincy and started tearing the meat apart. Jake offered the first piece to Quincy.

"This meat is not cooked enough and I don't eat with my hands."

Jake looked at the little man and said, "Suit yourself." He then laid the piece down on a rock close by and began eating his beans and meat. A short time later, Quincy got up from his seat on a rock and retrieved the piece of the hen. Before he was finished he ate all of the meat from the bones.

After they had eaten the meat, beans and some of the biscuits Jake brought out two tin cups from his saddle bags and filled them with coffee. He handed one to Quincy and sat at the foot of a small tree and sipped from his cup. After he drank the weak coffee he took the tin cups and washed them in the waterhole. Afterwards, Jake rolled a cigarette and stared off into the darkening skies. The little man interrupted him, "You really handled those fellows in the trading post. You must be a gun."

"Mister, I am not a gun. A gun is a killing tool, and we all would be better off if we didn't have them," replied Jake.

"No offense, Friend, I was just making conversation, besides, the dime novels always call people guns or gunmen."

Jake looked at the little man and said "No offense taken. You don't have food in that pack, what do you have?"

"As I was trying to explain to those other gents, I am a gun salesman from Colt Manufacturing Company," he said proudly.

"What is a gun salesman doing all the way from Connecticut?" asked Jake.

"At least you know something about the state of Connecticut."

"Mr. I know a lot about the state and got acquainted with many of the men from Connecticut during the war and even had to kill some of them."

"How did you know they were from Connecticut?"

"Because they were part of a Connecticut Regiment, so I assume that they were from Connecticut."

"Well, as I was saying, no offense but this is not just guns I am selling; they are the latest guns from Samuel Colt."

"I've heard the name, and I know weapons from Colt," replied Jake.

"What I am selling isn't just a weapon; it is the latest gun, the Colt 45."

"So you are telling me that you are traveling around the country with no food or water and trying to sell guns?"

"Sir, do you have a name?" asked Quincy.

"My name is Jake Harn."

"Oh yes, I remember you telling that man your name. Well, may I call you Jake? I hope we can be friends." Jake ignored him but Quincy continued anyway. "I just got off the train and started wandering, looking to sell guns and gather information for a book that I hope to write. The food and water was a mistake. I thought that

I would have plenty of chances to purchase supplies."

"Those kinds of mistakes will cause you to die from hunger or thirst or get you killed by Indians or outlaws."

"From where I came from we had food and water and didn't need to carry them. Also, we had laws and policemen to take care of ruffians such as those in the saloon."

"Quincy, you had better understand quickly that we have no law or policemen here to protect you and very few accommodations for strangers. You can ride for days without seeing a town or another person." Quincy for once was speechless, and Jake asked him, "This book you're going to write, what's it about?"

"Easterners are fascinated with the "wild west" and they are buying thousands of "dime novels" about gunfighters, marshals and other lawmen. I am planning to write one of these, except I want to write it about a real hero."

"And just where are you going to find one of these real, live, hero gunmen?" asked Jake as he snubbed out his cigarette.

"I was thinking as I rode today that I could model the hero after you," replied Quincy.

"Now I know you're crazy. I'm no gunman, and I'm no hero," said Jake.

"Well, you mentioned being in the war. That's a beginning. Then there's the way you handled yourself in

Willow Springs and the way that you shoot."

"No."

"Jake, I could polish up your image and ..."

"And create a whole other person. No thanks, Mr. Cranbrook. Go to sleep. I am going to check on the animals and I would suggest that you get as much rest as you can get because I will be up early in the morning if you plan to ride with me."

Jake walked over, picked up his rifle and headed toward the animals, which seemed contented enough for the night. When he came back he spread out his saddle blanket, took off his boots, and lay down with his pistol and rifle near his right hand. He could hear the little man muttering as he tried to get comfortable but Jake made no motion to help. Soon he was fast asleep.

Daylight found Jake awake and his first chore was to rekindle the fire to make coffee. He had a difficult time getting Quincy awake until he threatened to stick his head in the waterhole. Jake fixed a meager breakfast consisting of some leftover biscuits and slices of salted meat that he had in his saddle bags. Meager or not, the two men ate heartily and were finishing their coffee when the little man said, "Let me show you this new revolver, you might like it."

Jake looked skeptical and said, "I have a gun."

"But not a gun like this," replied Quincy.

Jake pulled out his Whitney Navy .36 caliber and showed it to Quincy. "This is a six shot pistol made by the Whitney Armory in Connecticut."

"I am familiar with the company."

"Sam Colt contracted Eli Whitney Jr. to build guns for his company. Later on the company started making its own weapons."

"Now you are telling me more than I need to know," said Jake.

"Just try it out and if you don't like it I will not bring it up again."

Jake hesitated and then replied "That, my friend is a deal. But make this quick, we should be on the road, we're burning daylight."

Quincy took a Colt 45 from his pack and handed it to Jake, who examined it carefully and asked, "You have any ammunition for this thing?"

Quincy hurried back to his pack and took out a box of shells and handed it to Jake. Jake loaded the gun and looked through the sites. He turned it over and studied it. "Good balance. Feels good."

"You'll like the way it shoots." The little man picked up a small rock and threw it a few yards away. "See if you can hit that."

The feel was a little different than that of the gun he was using, but Jake had had to adjust to many different guns. He took the Whitney out of the holster and handed it to Quincy. He then slipped the Colt 45 into the holster. He smoothly drew the gun and emptied it, hitting the rock every time.

"Wow, that's some shooting," said Quincy.

"Much obliged," replied Jake and attempted to hand the gun back to Quincy.

"Fifteen dollars for this remarkable gun," said Quincy.

"The one I have is good enough for me."

"Tell you what I will do, I'll give you the gun for helping me and if you carry it, others will see it and may want to buy one."

Jake thought about it for a moment. He sure liked this special gun. "Okay, I will take the gun, but I will have to keep my old one."

"Okay by me, I don't need it," replied Quincy.

Jake put the Whitney Navy in his saddlebag and re-loaded the 45. He slipped it in the holster and jerked it back out quickly and hit a smaller rock farther off. "Feels really good," he said.

The two men saddled up and rode out. Jake was very quiet as they rode but every now and again the little man asked questions about Jake or about the wild west that he had heard about while living in the East. Jake didn't want to be rude, so he answered his questions with as few words as he could get by with. Jake was flattered but he sure did not want the little man to write anything about him.

"How did you learn to shoot like that?" asked Quincy.

Jake knew that just cutting Quincy off would only

cause him to continue asking later so he answered. "When I left Georgia I met up with a wagon train and stayed with it for some time. I had a run-in with a Yankee. I tried to avoid trouble, but he continued to push the issue and finally he drew a gun on me. I shot and killed him."

Quincy interrupted him, "So, you were already fast with a gun?"

"No, and I was just lucky to beat the man because I had never had to draw and shoot at anyone or anything before. And besides I believe that the man had consumed more whiskey than he could handle. After that, the wagon master asked me to leave the train but before I left he suggested that I either take the gun off or get better with it before I got killed. I took his advice and spent many hours practicing the fast draw and hitting the target. In time it just became second nature to me."

"So, how do you stack up with Sam Bass, the Earp's, Doc Holliday and the other gunmen that they are writing books about?"

Jake was tired of the conversation so he replied, "Don't know any of them, ask them yourself." He was not exactly truthful because he had met Wyatt Earp and Doc Holliday in Dodge City. Holliday was a gambler and Earp was dealing Faro at the Long Branch Saloon and serving as Assistant City Marshall in Dodge at the time he met him. However, he was not about to tell Quincy, knowing he would never stop talking then.

Jake nudged his horse and rode on ahead.

Two

Jake Harn had left his last job with no idea where he was going. He had been drifting for some time and had spent many lonely days and nights on the trail. He had met only one other rider but they only spoke a dozen words or so before departing on their separate ways. Sleeping and eating on the trail often causes one to yearn to mingle with civilization, regardless of how uncivilized that civilization turns out to be. Just eating someone else's cooking or standing in front of the bar ordering a cold beer often eases the loneliness that always seems to be there.

Since he had no commitments, he figured that he would know when and where he would put down roots. The journey had been smooth except for yesterday's encounter at Willow Springs. Now he was riding with a companion. The ride should have been pleasant but the little man really irritated him. Quincy Cranbrook was nosey and chattered on endlessly.

Jake was used to sleeping on the trail but no matter how long he did it, the ground was still uncomfortable and the food did not taste like home cooking. It was early afternoon as the horse and rider topped a ridge. Unexpectedly a town appeared in the distance. Jake stopped his horse and built a smoke, inhaled deeply and surveyed the surroundings.

He looked at the sky and noticed that dark clouds were forming in the west and the breeze was picking up. Jake had been around long enough to know that those cloud formations usually meant heavy rain or wind storms. He was still thinking about the clouds when Cranbrook rode up on his donkey.

"Why are we riding so fast?" gasped the little man as if he was all out of breath.

Jake ignored him and moved his gaze toward the town on the horizon. He looked again at the dark clouds and decided that a smart man would seek shelter from the storm before it blew in.

It was still early afternoon, and Jake had intended to ride on a few miles but now he decided an overnight stop might be wise. He could eat and sleep in a real bed for the first time in a couple of weeks, and find shelter from the storm. He also thought about his horse, Muddy, who had been going for some time with short rations. Jake was no great shakes of a cook anyway but short supplies eliminated cooking altogether. Over the past few days he had existed on beef jerky, beans, water, and used coffee grounds. His supplies had pretty much run out a few days ago. He had hoped to stock up on supplies in Willow Springs but after his run-in with the bartender he decided that he would not be able to purchase anything. He was bone weary and a stop over to rest and re-supply himself would be good for both man and beast. In addition, he secretly hoped that he could leave Cranbrook at the next stop.

Some time later they rode their animals onto a dusty street and stopped in front of a wooden sign proclaiming, "You are entering Burkeville." A few feet ahead was another sign noting that the street itself was "Main Street." It appeared that the town had only two streets. Main Street consisted of a saloon, hotel, general store, gunsmith, livery stable, barber shop and a few houses. Next to the livery stable sign was a smaller sign indicating Baxter Stage Line. The other street crossed Main but Jake could not see the layout from this vantage point. He rode on and stopped his horse at the water trough, allowing Muddy to drink. Quincy started to ride on but the donkey he was riding automatically brought his rider to the trough in spite of his rider's objections.

Jake really hankered for a cold beer, but he knew that having the horse ready to go in the morning was much more important than a drink from the saloon for the rider. After the horse had drunk his fill, Jake guided him to a hitch rail in front of the Trail's End Saloon. Next to the saloon was Burkeville General Mercantile and attached to the Mercantile was the telegraph office. He reined in and sat in the saddle for a few moments. Jake thought to himself that the name "Mercantile" was quite a mouth full in such a small town. General store would have been more accurate.

Being a cautious person by nature, Jake surveyed his surroundings before dismounting. The swinging doors of the saloon were inviting him in, but this was a strange town and Jake had learned by experience to be careful and know as much as he could before walking into saloons. As he looked up and down the street he noticed nothing unusual. His practiced eyes stopped on three cowboys who were talking and lounging a few feet away. They stopped their conversation and stared at Jake. The gent in the middle of the trio stood out from the other two. He was tall, handsome, controlled the conversation and appeared to be very young. In addition he also stood out from the other cowboys because of his dress and the fancy six shooters that he wore. They were tied down low on his hips indicating that he was a gunman. The other two gents didn't appear to be ordinary cowpokes. They did not dress as fancy as the young gunman but neither did their dress match that of the typical cowboy.

Jake stepped down from his horse, loosened the cinch and took out the Henry repeating rifle from the boot of his saddle. Force of habit caused him to carry the rifle when he left his horse. Jake was familiar with other common rifles used in the war but he was partial to the Henry. The Henry rifle was invented by Benjamin Tyler Henry. A Confederate officer had said of it, "It's a rifle that you can load on Sunday and shoot all week long." The rapid and highly accurate fire was in part due to the .44 caliber rim fire metallic cartridges that it used. It had a magazine with 15 cartridges compared to the more common Spencer Carbine that held only seven cartridges. The Spencer was standard U.S. Cavalry issue at the end of the war. The Henry could fire 15 shots within 11 seconds while the Spencer took about 20 seconds to fire 7 rounds. Both of these rifles were used by the North and the South but most of the Henry's were purchased by the individual soldiers or the states rather than the federal governments.

Jake cleared his thoughts and patted the horse on his forehead. The horse shook his head as though he did not like the attention but then he playfully nudged his master as Jake turned to walk away toward the saloon, rifle in hand.

His horse, Muddy, was a rangy bay with three white stockings. With the white stockings it appeared as he had been walking in mud so Jake called him Muddy. Jake had paid hard cash for him at one of his many stops. The previous owner had given up ever taming him and was willing to part with him for less than the market price. Jake worked with him for a while but decided that he was not going to be tamed. However, he found that the two could and eventually did arrive at an uneasy truce. Jake found out that even though the horse was playful at times, he was downright ornery at other times. Jake put up with him because he had more than average stamina and had proven to be surefooted on the trail.

Jake had forgotten about Quincy but he noticed as he reached the porch that the little man had ridden on toward the hotel. As Jake stepped inside the saloon he stopped to allow his eyes to become accustomed to the darkness and to familiarize himself with the room. On his left were several tables, mostly empty. Apparently it was too early for the crowd because only three cowboys were in the room sitting at a table. They were playing poker and nursing glasses of rye whiskey. On his right was a bar that was nothing fancy, but like many others on the trail, it served its purpose. The bartender was a heavy-set gentleman wearing an apron. Jake stepped up to the bar and the bartender approached him.

"What'll you have, Stranger?" he asked.

"Right now a beer and some information, replied Jake."

"The beer is easy, don't know about the information."

"Looks like a storm coming, some food and a bed for the night would be enough for me," Jake replied as he laid his rifle on the bar.

"We don't serve food here, but I can direct you to the café. It's open, and the only restaurant in town," said the bartender as he set a foamy mug of beer in front of Jake. "The café is right down the street and across from the Burkeville Hotel. You can't miss it."

"Much obliged," answered Jake. Before he took a drink, he glanced toward the saloon door just as the three men from the sidewalk entered.

The tall handsome gent, who appeared to be the leader of the group stepped closer and looked directly at Jake. "What's your name, and what's your business in Burkeville?" he asked.

Jake knew a town bully when he saw one, and he braced for trouble. Before answering, he took a long drink from his beer mug and put it back on the bar. "Jake, what's yours?"

"Everybody in town already knows my name and I don't answer to strangers."

"If you tell me your name then we won't be strangers."

"Never mind about me, just answer the question. We don't welcome strangers in Burkeville," retorted the man.

Jake was tired from the ride and irritated by Quincy and pissed off by the situation at Willow Springs yesterday. He was in no mood to be friendly. He looked at the man evenly and asked, "Who are these people that don't welcome strangers?"

"Mister, I'm asking the questions, and I'd suggest that you state your business and ride out before you get more trouble than you can handle," replied the man.

Even though a storm was likely coming, Jake didn't

have his heart set on staying in Burkeville. It was the tone of the man's voice that convinced him he would stay over. Jake replied, "Friend, I will tell you one time just to avoid trouble even though it's against my better judgment. I am going to eat, sleep in a real bed, and leave early in the morning, if that is satisfactory to you?"

"You're trying my patience and nothing you say is going to be to my likin', and I say that you're leaving today," snarled the angry gent. It was apparent to Jake that this gunman was used to getting his way in Burkeville.

The bartender looked at him and said, "Sonny, leave the man alone and get out of my saloon. Go home – you've had too much to drink."

The man called Sonny glared at the bartender and said, "Stay out of my business or I will be gunning for you next."

"I and the rest of the town have stayed out of your business since you came back to town and, me for one, am sorry that I did," replied the barkeep.

Sonny ignored the bartender's remarks, looked at Jake and said, "Well, what's it going to be?"

Jake deliberately finished his beer and looked at Sonny. "I'm going to repeat myself one more time because apparently you don't understand. When I leave here I'm going to the café down the street, eat my fill, find a room in the hotel and then turn in for the night."

Sonny looked at his two friends. One nodded his head yes, as if to show approval, and the other appeared to be completely indifferent to what was going on. Sonny assumed his friends would back his play so he looked back at Jake. "We'll drag you out feet first if necessary."

"Boy, I strongly advise you not to pull on me," Jake's voice was ice cold.

"Don't call me boy. Even my father don't call me boy."

Jake stared at Sonny but said nothing.

Looking in those cold, blue eyes of the stranger he hesitated a moment but continued, "You're going to die if you don't leave town," hissed Sonny.

"We all die, some before their time," replied Jake.

Sonny cussed at Jake and said, "You're going to die now!"

Jake edged away from the bar and faced Sonny saying, "Well, I guess that's the way it's going to be. You have a gun; you may as well use it."

Sonny looked at Jake, laughed, and said, "The Bar B will pay for your coffin."

"Very kind of you, I'm grateful," replied Jake sarcastically.

Sonny did not like the cockiness of the stranger but he was damn sure that he was not going to back down now. His reputation in Burkeville was too important for that.

Sonny feinted to his left, hunched over, and suddenly clawed at his guns. The right hand gun came out of the holster and came up but he never got a chance to fire it. The left hand gun never cleared leather. Jake read the feint correctly, moved quickly, whipped out his new 45 and fired. He only fired once, but that was enough. His bullet hit Sonny in the chest, driving him backwards. He lost his balance and crashed to the floor. His gun was still in his right hand but he would never use it again.

Jake looked around the room, but the two friends of Sonny quickly distanced themselves from the fight. The cowboys at the table watched curiously and continued sipping their drinks. Shootings apparently were not that uncommon in Burkeville.

Sonny's companions quickly left the saloon and the bartender hollered at one of the men at the table, "Rusty, go fetch the sheriff."

"Aw, leave him there Pat, Burkes men will come for him soon enough when those two gents tell Burke," he answered.

"Get the Sheriff!" shouted the bartender. Rusty muttered a few obscenities as he slowly walked out the door toward the sheriff's office.

The bartender looked at Jake and said, "You'll want to skip the food and shelter and move on down the trail quickly, the man you shot is Sonny Burke."

"And I'm supposed to be impressed?" asked Jake.

"Well, Sonny is, or was I should say, one of the sons of the largest and most powerful rancher in this whole territory. He really did not do much work on the ranch, but the old man adored him anyway. He backed him even when his son killed an unarmed man over at Jones Crossing. Jeff Burke reportedly paid off, or scared off, the judge and Sonny got off scot free. Burke has two other sons, but he always favored Sonny," answered the bartender.

"Why would this Sonny want to pick on a total stranger?"

"He was the town bully and because of his father, most folks stayed clear of him and the ones that didn't are buried in boot hill, west of town."

"And the sheriff?"

"He makes himself scarce when issues come up about the Burkes."

"Scared?"

"Too many guns for one man."

"How about the other two brothers?" asked Jake.

"Well, Matt's the youngest and he is the least like old man Burke. He's also interested in the lady at the hotel. The oldest brother is Clay. He is much like the old man, and he does whatever his dad wants him to do," said the bartender.

Just as the bartender finished, the sheriff strode in with Rusty following close behind. "What happened here?" asked the sheriff.

Before anyone else could say anything, the bartender said, "Sonny tried to run this man out of town but he finally tangled with someone that chose not to take his advice."

"When he wouldn't budge, Sonny tried to gun him down," added Rusty.

One of the other cowboys at the table spoke up, "Sheriff, it was a fair fight, Sonny simply met his match this time, but I still wouldn't want to be in this fellar's shoes when the Burkes find out Sonny is dead."

The sheriff nodded toward Jake and said, "Even so, I will have to take you in for questioning. Let me have your guns."

"I don't want to seem unfriendly, Sheriff, but I don't give up my guns to anyone," responded Jake.

The bartender chimed in, "Sheriff, you have no call to arrest this man. Everyone here saw what happened and they know that it was self-defense. Sonny has been bullying people in this town since he was a kid and this time he simply ran up against someone that didn't back down."

The sheriff looked at Jake and noticed the cold, steel, blue eyes staring back at him. He decided that discretion was the better part of valor and, besides, the Burkes could take care of this situation themselves. "Just don't leave town until I get to the bottom of this," growled the sheriff as he turned and walked out the door.

After the sheriff left, the bartender looked at Jake

and said, "Take my advice and move on quickly; the Burkes have a way of finding out everything that happens in town when it happens and they will be in town, in mass, before midnight. I am not sure who the other gents were with Sonny but I suspect they are new hands from the Bar B Ranch."

"I appreciate your concern, but I'm tired, hungry and I don't want to get caught in the storm that's blowing in," replied Jake as he moved toward the door. "Besides, my horse is tired and he wouldn't be able to outrun Burkes men with their fresh horses."

Jake looked at the bartender and said, "Thanks for everything, Pat."

"Just you be careful, many people in town owe allegiance to the Burkes."

As he walked out the door, Jake thought he was probably a fool for staying but he had been in trouble many times before. He was not looking for trouble, but he was not in the habit of running from it. Even though he was born to a plantation owner in Georgia, his life had been far from easy. His family owned large holdings on the Ogeechee River, several miles south of Savannah, and it was operated by the family with help from slaves and hired men. The plantation shipped tons of cotton to the mills and the warehouses in the river city.

It was hard physical labor, and Jake was required to work even harder than the helpers. His background kept his feet on the ground when his friends were shipped off to schools up north. Jake harbored no grudge against his friends because they went away to school. His education in Savannah was good from an academic standpoint and the hard work and physical education that taught him to defend himself.

When war broke out Jake felt duty calling and enlisted in the Confederate Army early on. He initially joined Company A of the First Georgia Infantry. His first duty was to help in the construction of a fort on the Ogeechee River, about fifteen miles from Savannah to help defend the city. The fort later came to be known as Fort McAllister, after Captain Joseph McAllister who commanded the fort and owned the land where it was built. After Fort McAllister, Jake served in several campaigns including Cold Harbor and Antietam. He was privileged to serve with the great Confederate soldier Major General J.E.B. Stuart. Jake was wounded several times during his enlistment, but his wounds had all healed before his discharge at the end of the war. He went in as a captain, mainly because of his father's influence, and had been discharged as a major.

Jake shook these memories and cleared his mind and thought about the Burkes. As bad as they might be they could not match the hell that he had already been through. He moved out onto the porch. He felt the strong wind that was blowing in and saw the dust swirling in the street. Jake looked at the sky and knew the clouds that he had seen earlier were going to open up soon.

Three

Jake took Muddy to the livery stable before heading to the café. The livery man was just inside the door working on a saddle.

"Hello, Friend," said Jake. "Need to get some care for my horse."

The man glanced at Jake and said, "My name's Jed, and you came to the right place."

"Do you have a last name Jed?" asked Jake.

"Iffen' I did I've plumb forgotten it. Folks around town jus' call me Old Jed."

"Okay, Old Jed, my name is Jake Harn, and how about a stall for my horse?"

"No problem a'tall," Old Jed answered.

Jake ordered an extra helping of oats and some hay for Muddy and asked that he be bedded down in a comfortable stall. He told Old Jed that he would be leaving early in the morning and he wanted the horse fresh for the trip. He took his saddle bags and rifle, waved to Old Jed, then walked the two blocks to the café to take care of his own hunger.

The café consisted of six tables with rough lumber chairs and a kitchen in the back that was almost hidden from the customers. An elderly couple occupied one of the tables and the only other customer was Lattimore Q. Cranbrook. He assumed that business was slow because it was so early in the evening. Jake took a seat at the corner table with his back to the wall and laid his saddle bags on the floor next to the table. He had a habit of watching the door when he was in strange places. After a few moments a short, squat lady came out of the kitchen and waddled toward the table.

"What'll you have?" she asked, sounding as if she was completely disinterested.

"Coffee, steak and potatoes," replied Jake.

"Ain't got no steak today," she answered.

"Well, what would you suggest?" he asked.

"The only thing we have right now is beef stew," she answered.

"Well then, I'll have beef stew, bread and coffee," replied Jake.

"It'll take me a while to get it," she said as she waddled off toward the kitchen. The elderly couple was listening to the exchange, but when Jake looked over their way they quickly turned back to their food.

Mr. Cranbrook finished his coffee and sidled up to the table.

"Mr. Harn, you created some excitement without me," he said.

"Quincy, I did not create any excitement. It just happened."

The little man looked at Jake admiringly and asked,

"May I join you?"

Jake motioned for him to sit, but he ignored Quincy's attempt to gather information about the shooting.

It took a while but the waitress came from the kitchen with a piping hot plate of stew, a steaming cup of coffee and a large slice of sourdough bread.

"Plenty more stew," she told him, "and plenty of coffee."

"Thank you but I'm not sure that I will need any more stew," he said as he sipped the hot coffee. The coffee was good but the stew had very little beef and not much flavor. Nevertheless, Jake cleaned his plate and sopped up the remainder with the bread. The waitress came back with more coffee and Jake rocked back in his chair to relax and enjoy the second cup.

"Well, Mr. Harn, I sent a wire to the home office and I got a reply. They want me to proceed on to Dodge City, so I will be on the early morning stage," said the little man.

Jake continued to sip his coffee and he nodded, "Have a good trip."

Quincy stood up and started to walk away. "By the way, Mr. Harn, I will be back to talk about our earlier discussion." Jake ignored him and he walked out the door.

A few minutes later, the door opened and in walked the most beautiful woman that Jake had ever seen. He had been around southern women and many of them were beautiful but none compared to this creature. She was tall, had long brown hair and skin as smooth as silk. She wore a green dress with faint threads of gold in it. The dress clung to her ample breasts and her firm shoulders. She glanced at Jake but spoke to the waitress. "Johnny, we are having several guests at the hotel, and they have requested that they be seated and eat as a group."

Jake looked at the woman and at Johnny. This was the first time he had heard the name of the waitress. Johnny was an unusual name, but Jake was not concerned about her. His mind was on the angel that had just come into his life.

At that moment the angel turned to Jake and said coldly, "I thought you would've left town by this time."

"Have we met?" asked Jake.

"We haven't met but I know who you are. Everyone in town now knows your name."

"And then why should I have been gone?" he asked with a twinkle in his eye.

"If you are in town when the Bar B hands come in with Mr. Burke you'll be sorry that you decided to stay," replied the woman.

"Well, I am here because I was really hungry and besides I heard that Johnny here has the best food in town," he replied, "and I didn't want to miss it."

Johnny stared at him for a moment and said, "Go

on, everyone knows this is the only café in town." She looked back at the lady and said, "Certainly, Sarah, we can seat your guests together if they come early."

"Thank you, Johnny," she said, as she glanced at Jake and quickly left the café.

Johnny looked at Jake and said, "So, you're the man that killed that spoiled, young, man in the saloon. I'm sure that you had good reason to do it but it won't matter with old man Burke. He adored this one, even though everyone knew that he was no good."

Jake drained his coffee cup, stood and stretched. It felt good to have a belly full of food and strong coffee. Jake was just a shade over six feet, lean hips and broad shoulders. He was thirty-one years old and powerfully built. He had dark brown hair and cold, blue eyes that seemed to look through everyone.

Jake looked at Johnny and said, "Thanks for the grub and I really meant it. I have not eaten this good in a couple of weeks." He flipped a coin to her, nodded, and turned toward the door.

"You're just saying that 'cause you probably have been on the trail for a couple of weeks," she shouted as he went through the door and into the street.

The rain had begun to fall and Jake wondered if the rain would delay the arrival of Burke and his men. He decided that if what he heard about the old man were true the rain would not stop him. Jake shook his head and walked on.

Four

Jake walked out of the café with his stomach full and a gnawing conviction that trouble was brewing on the horizon. He headed toward the hotel, paying close attention to what was going on in the street. The wind was still blowing and large raindrops fell onto the dusty street. There was no sign of trouble as he reached the hotel door, so he walked in.

He was startled, but very pleased, to find that the beautiful woman from the café was in the lobby. She had company and did not pay any attention to Jake when he walked toward the desk.

"Yes, Sir, what can I do for you?" asked the clerk.

"I would like a room, preferably on the front, facing the street," answered Jake, as he dropped his saddlebags and the rifle on the counter.

"Yes, Sir, I believe that we can accommodate you. Do you have any luggage?"

"Just what you see," replied Jake.

The desk clerk handed him a key for room seven and as Jake turned to go he noticed the woman staring at him intently, her eyes full of hostility.

As he started for the stairs, she walked up to him with ice in her voice and said, "I see that you've chosen to ignore all the warnings about leaving town."

"Well, good evening to you, Miss Sarah," remarked Jake.

"If you please, I would prefer that you call me Miss Garnett," she retorted, "and you did not answer my question."

"Well, Miss Garnett, I appreciate you and all the friendly town folks urging me to get out of town but I believe that morning will suit me better," he replied.

"Mister whatever-your-name-is, you don't understand about the Burkes. The men that ride for the ranch are powerful and ruthless and they control almost everything and everyone in and around this town. They may decide to burn this town down to the ground to get you. Would you please take your problems somewhere else?" she pleaded.

"Ma'am, you can call me Jake, and does that include this hotel?" asked Jake.

"What are you talking about?" she asked angrily.

"The Burkes. Do they own this hotel?"

"I own this hotel, and I do not want it damaged by the Burkes because of you," she shouted.

"Miss Garnett, I really appreciate your concern but I am not leaving until morning, assuming that the coming storm has blown over by that time," he said.

"Well, you…you pigheaded fool," she stammered as she turned on her heels and walked away.

Jake watched as she hurried away. Just as she left

the hotel lobby, he remembered the conversation with the bartender. Matt Burke is seeing the lady at the hotel, he had said. Jake wondered if she was the woman he was talking about. His interest in her did not wane just because of the possible link to young Burke.

Jake's thoughts went back to the Burkes. If there was to be a confrontation he wanted to be ready. He was carrying his rifle and his six-gun but a little more fire power would make him more comfortable. From what he had heard, the Burkes would come in bunches and a shotgun might come in handy. Mobs could be better persuaded, he knew, with a scattergun. There was a gunsmith only a couple doors down from the hotel, and he decided to visit him before turning in for the night.

The shop was empty except for an older man behind the counter working on a pistol. He greeted Jake as he approached the counter. "Going to get some rain. You better stay close to your slicker. I was just getting ready to close, my wife expects me to be home for supper on time every day."

"Well," Jake replied, "I'll try and not keep you and your supper very long."

"In that case, my name is Virgil Johnson. What can I do for you, Mister?" he asked.

Jake replied, "Well, Sir, I need a shotgun and a box of shells."

"Wait a minute," the clerk said, and stared at Jake for

a moment. "You're the man who killed Sonny Burke in the saloon this afternoon, ain't you?"

"Sorry to say, it'd be me," said Jake.

"Listen, Mister, if the Burkes find out that I sold you a shotgun I'll not be able to live in this town. That is, if they don't shoot me first," he said.

"I wouldn't want to be responsible for your death, but I sure need that scatter gun," answered Jake.

"Well, maybe this town does not have a very healthy climate to live in anyway, and it would be nice if someone could take on the Burkes. I do have a double barrel shotgun that I will sell you, and I'll even throw in the shells," he told Jake.

"Much obliged," Jake said. He counted out the money, took the shotgun—a double barrel Greener. He wrapped the gun and the shells in his coat.

"Mister, are you familiar with this gun?"

"I have had a lot of experience with this model. Some folks consider it the best shotgun ever made. Thanks again," he said as he turned to go.

"Good luck. You'll certainly need it. By the way, I didn't catch your name," said the gunsmith.

"Jake . . . . Jake Harn," he answered.

"Glad to know you, Mr. Harn, and I hope we see you later."

"So do I," said Jake with a weak smile.

His new purchase in hand, Jake walked out the door and onto the sidewalk. The mercantile was just next door, and Jake decided to get some tobacco. Tomorrow he would load up on supplies before he pulled out, but for now, he needed the tobacco. He walked in the store and noticed that there were no other customers. A middle-aged man and woman were working behind the counter and Jake decided that they must be husband and wife. The man greeted Jake and said, "I don't believe that I've seen you in here before. My name is Clem Stratton. My wife and I own the store. What can I do for you?"

"Just some smokes for now," replied Jake as he handed him a list. "Can you please fill this order? I will pick it up early in the morning." Jake handed him a fairly extensive list.

Clem Stratton studied the list a moment and said, "I think we can fill this okay."

"Much obliged."

Clem brought the tobacco and said, "Don't see many strangers in town. Are you just passing through?"

"Trying to," answered Jake.

"Well, the store opens at seven a.m. sharp and the supplies will be ready."

Jake avoided saying much because he didn't want anyone else to ask questions about the killing in the saloon. "Much obliged and good night," said Jake as he headed to the door.

Jake returned to the hotel porch, rolled a smoke and took a few deep drags. The wind had slowed down and the rain was falling steadily. His eyes scanned the street, which appeared to be almost deserted except for some commotion inside the saloon. When he was satisfied that there was no immediate trouble he ground the butt under his heel and headed for the door. He walked into the hotel and climbed the stairs to the second floor. Everyone probably knows I am here, he thought, but there is no reason to flaunt it. His room was two doors down on the left. He checked the hallway to make sure that he knew where the exits were before heading to his room. He turned the key in the door and the door squeaked but opened easily. He noted the squeak and decided that it might come in handy if any unwanted visitors tried to come into the room.

Jake surveyed the room. Typical hotel room: a bed, one chair and a table with a pail of water and a wash basin. Jake laid the shotgun, shells, and the Henry on the bed and dropped his saddle bags on the floor near the bed. He then unbuckled his gun belt and hung it over the bed post. He poured water into the basin and cleaned himself up as much as he could without a bath tub. He considered ordering a bath but discarded the notion and instead decided to take a nap.

He stretched out on the bed fully clothed, hoping for a quick nap. He soon dozed off. Jake was normally a light sleeper, but this time when he heard the banging on the door he was groggy and still half asleep. He was slow to respond and at first he was not sure that he had even gone to sleep. The person outside the room knocked louder and shouted, "Wake up! The Burkes are here and they are demanding to see you."

As he understood what the man was saying the realization hit him that he had slept much longer than he had planned to. Jake recognized the voice of the desk clerk and he sounded frantic. Jake got out of bed, pulled the Colt 45 out of the holster and opened the door a crack just as the clerk started to knock on the door again.

"Calm down," Jake said, "you will wake everyone in the hotel." His tone was sarcastic.

"Mister, thank God you opened the door. Old man Burke says he is going to burn the hotel if you don't come down," he shouted. Then lowered his voice, "I'm sorry to bother you because I really don't care much for the Burkes, but, well, you understand."

"That's okay. Just tell them that I will be down shortly," he said wryly. The desk clerk nodded and hurried down the stairs with the message. Jake went to the wash basin, splashed some cold water on his face, buckled on his gun, and picked up the shotgun. He reached for his hat but decided not to take it. He figured he certainly did not have to worry about the sun in his eyes. He loaded the shotgun and checked the trigger mechanism. He wanted to make sure that it went off when he wanted it to go off.

He went down the stairs and noticed that several

people were anxiously looking out the windows. He found his mind and eyes searching for Sarah but she was no place to be seen. He did see Quincy looking out a window. He nodded at Jake when their eyes met.

Jake lifted his pistol out of the holster, checked the loads and allowed it to slide back in. The gun felt good in his hand. He wondered if he should have gone back to his old gun but discarded the notion. Jake then cocked the hammers on the shotgun and cuddled it in his left arm before walking out the door and onto the sidewalk. The rain was still falling but had eased up from earlier. Even so, there was enough wind to drive the rain drops back toward the riders. It allowed Jake to see the men better than they could see Jake, and he fully intended to take any advantage that he could get.

Jake looked at the crowd, finally settling his eyes on what had to be Jeff Burke. He sat on a big black horse with an English saddle and fancy trimmings. He was tall, about Jake's size, with a white mustache and fancy clothing. Jake surveyed the large crowd closer but did not see anyone that he recognized. Many of the people were just bystanders but others were fully armed and mounted. The bartender told him that Burke had two other sons, and Jake assumed the two men flanking Burke were those sons. The one on the right had to be Clay Burke because of his remarkable resemblance to old man Burke. The other appeared to be around twenty-one years old.

A gent from the back spoke up, "That's him, Mr. Burke, that's the one that gunned down Sonny." Jake did not see the man but recognized the voice as belonging to one of the men that had been in the saloon with Sonny Burke.

Jeff Burke, with a booming voice, shouted to Jake, "Harn, I have come to take my son home and drop you off at Boot Hill."

"Sorry to disappoint you, Mr. Burke, but I'm not going that way," replied Jake.

"You're trying to run a bluff, and I'm telling you that it's not going to work," shouted Burke.

"Mr. Burke, I don't bluff. Now I am sorry that your son got killed, but it was self-defense and everyone there saw it," replied Jake. "It was him or me, and he lost."

"Mister, it does not matter whether you are sorry or not and it doesn't matter if you say self-defense. My son is dead and you're going to have to pay for his death," retorted Burke.

"Mr. Burke, I will be glad to leave this town early tomorrow morning and never come back, but right now I'm going to spend the night in this hotel. I'm not looking for a fight."

"Harn, you're not going to be able to avoid a fight," replied Burke.

"Burke, if you insist on a fight you may as well get

on with it but I'm telling you that you're going to get a lot of people killed in the process," said Jake as he lifted the Greener to shoulder level.

The men at the front recognized the shotgun in his hands and tried to back up but to no avail, the others were too close.

Burke, feeling that he might lose the crowd, went on the offense. "Mister, I have twenty guns here, and I can do anything that I want to do, including taking this town apart," shouted Burke.

From Jake's battle-hardened days he had learned to stay cool in order to make better decisions. "Apparently you already own most of the town and the people in it," said Jake. "You may as well take it apart."

"Time to talk is over, Harn. Let's get it over with," shouted Burke.

"Burke, as you can see, I have a double barreled shotgun cocked, and a twitch of my finger will blast you and everyone around you to kingdom come. At fifteen feet, there is no way that I can miss, and you will be the first person dead," declared Jake.

"Let's get him," shouted a man from the back.

It was dark, but the lights from the hotel gave off enough light to allow Burke to see the shotgun pointed right at him. He was a smart man and no fool when it came to guns. "Shut up, Slim," replied Burke "You're not in the line of fire and I'm still running the show."

"You all may want to consider your options quickly

because I may not be able to keep my trigger finger still much longer," said Jake.

The younger man on the left of Burke leaned over and said something to Burke that Jake could not catch, but he did see Burke's reaction. He obviously was unhappy with what appeared to be his younger son's suggestion.

The old man stared at Jake for a short while then shouted, "You may have won this round but the battle isn't over. I promise you that you will not get out of this territory alive. I'm personally providing a grave for you at Boot Hill."

"Mr. Burke, this is the second time that I have been offered a space in Boot Hill but again, I am declining your generous offer, and I'll be glad to shed the dust of this town in the morning as I leave," said Jake.

Burke's glare was full of hate as he spoke. "Leaving town is not good enough for you. Just remember what I said." Then he called out to his men, "Let's go, Boys; we'll finish this job later."

Jake eased off the trigger as he watched Burke and the others head toward the undertaker's office. He needed a cup of coffee, but he noticed that the café was dark. He considered going to the saloon for a drink but he decided that might be too risky. He turned and walked back into the hotel and almost ran into Sarah, who was standing just inside the door.

"Mr. Harn, if you think that grandstanding will get

you out of town safely you're sadly mistaken," said Sarah. "Burke has money and men, and he can buy whatever he wants or needs to get rid of you. You heard him say that he'll take the town apart. You should have taken the advice and left town when you had the chance."

"Why, Miss Garnett, I do believe that you are worried about me," he stated sarcastically.

"Mr. Harn . . . " she started to speak.

But Jake interrupted her. "Call me Jake."

"Mr. Harn," she started again, "you must have a higher opinion of yourself than I do because I am only concerned about this town and the safety of its people," she said as she turned and angrily walked away.

"Ma'am, if you are so concerned about the town folks, ask them stand up to Burke."

Sarah stopped, stared at Jake, stomped her foot and stalked off.

Jake watched her walk away shook his head and started walking back upstairs to his room. From behind him came the squeaky voice of Lattimore Q. Cranbrook, "You sure showed them, didn't you?"

Jake looked over his shoulder at the little man and said, "I sure did," as he continued up the stairs without stopping.

When Jake got in the room he took the only chair and propped it against the door enough so that it would not come completely open. He then rolled his bed covers up on the bed to look like a person sleeping, took off his boots and gun, blew out the lamp, and lay down to sleep on the floor behind the bed. He dozed off quickly. Some time later he awoke with a start. He heard something and quickly realized it was the squeaky door. Jake had allowed the door to be opened just enough for it to squeak.

Just as he reached for his gun, two quick shots hit the bed covers. Jake snapped a quick shot at the door, heard a yelp, then footsteps fading down the hall. He quickly moved to the door and cautiously opened it. He stepped into the hall but no one was there. He lit the hall lamp that had been put out and looked for a shell casing but no luck. What he did see was a few drops of fresh blood in the hall. It had to have been left by the shooter as he fled along the hall and down the stairs.

He went back to the room, poured water into the wash basin and washed his face. He dried off with a towel and looked out of the window. The sun would be coming up soon. He began packing his belongings for his departure. When he finished he went downstairs and saw that the clerk was dozing at the desk. He decided not to wake him but instead, walked to the café for coffee.

The rain had stopped falling and the morning was clear, crisp, and quiet. When Jake walked into the café he saw that the only person there was Johnny. She was preparing biscuits and salt pork for the crowd that would soon arrive for breakfast. "Good morning," she greeted Jake, "I heard that you had an interesting visit with Mr. Burke last evening."

Jake decided that her attitude toward him had changed since yesterday. It could have been because of the altercation last night, he thought.

"That wasn't all," he replied. "Afterwards someone took a shot at me while I was in the hotel room."

"Mister, you know that Burke is not going to let you out of the territory alive! Especially since you killed his son and humiliated him and his gunmen. Well, what would you like to eat?" she asked.

"Plenty of coffee and whatever grub you can rustle up quickly," he answered.

"Men--- all you think about is feeding your mouth when you should be thinking about how to save your hide." She hurried off to the kitchen to get the food.

Soon she came back with a plate of eggs, ham, biscuits and a steaming hot cup of coffee. "Eat up," she said, "This may be your last meal."

Jake grinned at her and replied, "I certainly hope not."

A few customers started drifting in as he finished off the breakfast and drained the last of the second cup of coffee. He counted out some coins and gave them to her to pay for the food. When he begin to leave she said, "You know, Burke's men will be guarding the main road out of town."

Well, do you have a better suggestion?" he asked with a halfway grin.

"You may want to go past the Sterling Ranch rather than the main road. The Sterling's are much friendlier and they might help you get safely out of the territory."

"Thank you, Johnny. How would I find this ranch?" he asked.

"Just go west on the main road about a mile and take the left fork for about three miles and you can't miss it," she said.

"Much obliged, Johnny, and thanks for your help and the grub," he answered then added, "By the way, how did you get to be here in this God-forsaken town?"

"I came with my good-for-nothing husband. He was going to be a big rancher, but he either drank up or spent on women everything that he ever earned. I worked at the hotel and Miss Garnett loaned me the money to open this place," she replied.

"If you don't mind my asking, where is your husband now?"

"He's dead. Supposedly got drunk and fell off his horse and hit his head on a rock. There are others that believe that he was killed by a jealous husband and made out like it was an accident. Either way it don't matter."

"I'm sorry that it didn't work out," said Jake.

She looked at Jake and with a chuckle she said, "Well,

if you are really sorry find me another husband."

Jake waved at her and as he turned to go he said with a smile, "I'll keep my eyes open."

Jake left the café and went back to his room to gather his belongings. Downstairs, he paid his bill and went to the general store. His supplies were ready so he paid for them, said goodbye to the store owner, and walked directly to the stable. There was no one around so he saddled Muddy and walked him out of the livery stable. He stored the supplies in the saddle bags and put the Henry in the scabbard. He kept the shotgun cradled in his left arm. He looked up and down the street, but it was almost empty. His instincts were aroused when he thought he saw a man duck back into the alley by the hotel. He looked again but saw nothing so he put it out of his mind, stepped in the saddle and rode west.

The darkness was fading as the light of day began to illuminate the sky. Jake figured that by leaving early he would avoid part of the hot sun that would beat down on the land later on in the day. He also hoped that he could avoid any Burke men that may be still in town. He was not in a hurry riding out of town. He decided that although he was concerned about the Burkes, he might need a rested horse later, so he allowed Muddy to take his time. Several minutes of easy riding saw them at the fork in the road that Johnny had told him about. He sat on the horse for a few minutes and rolled a cigarette as he surveyed the surroundings. As he glanced left he saw a small sign with an arrow and the words, "Sterling Ranch three miles." Going straight could save a few miles, he thought, but being in safer territory might be more important. He decided to take Johnny's advice and take the left fork to the Sterling Ranch. He put out the cigarette and turned Muddy towards the left fork.

A creek murmured off to Jake's left as he rode toward the Sterling Ranch. He decided to stop off and take a much-needed bath. He had hoped to get a hot bath in Burkeville but circumstances made that impossible. He guided Muddy off the road and pulled up near a shallow pool of water.

Jake laid the shotgun close by and lay belly-flat in the water and drank upstream of the bay; he let the horse loose at a nearby grassy spot to graze while he built another smoke. He stretched out in a shady spot under a willow and contemplated the day's activities. After some moments he put out the smoke and got out his shaving gear and soap. He chose a deeper part of the stream, slipped off his clothes and stepped into the water. The water was cold but it provided a soothing feeling that Jake had not had lately. He was just about to dry off when Muddy raised his head and his ears pricked toward a wooded area a few yards away. His horse was a good watch-dog and his neighing probably meant that another horse was around. Jake dried off, quickly dressed, picked up the shotgun, caught his horse, mounted, and headed on toward the Sterling Ranch.

He had only been riding a short while when the hair on his neck began to rise. He had a feeling that someone, or someones, were not far away. Jake had learned to heed his instincts because they were usually right. He prodded Muddy to pick up the pace, but he was careful not to spook anyone riding nearby. After riding for only a short time he saw a dust cloud far down the road. He spoke gently to Muddy, "We may have company so be ready to run."

Just about that time, he heard a rifle shot, felt a stab of pain in his left shoulder and felt Muddy jerk forward. Jake lost his grip on the reins that he held in his left hand and he began falling. He was aware that he hit something and then everything went black.

Five

As he became conscious Jake felt like he was in a fog. He shook his head to try and clear the cobwebs but with limited success. He hurt all over. He could hear faint voices but he couldn't recognize any of them. After struggling to understand what was going on he could make out a voice. It said, "He's coming to . . . ."

Jake tried to turn his head toward the voice but the pain was too great. He had no idea where he was or who the people were speaking and moving about the room. Someone said, "It's too damn bad that he's not dead, I'm sure he's one of Burkes men."

Another man asked, "Then why would he be on this road? Only locals would even know that this goes beyond the ranch."

"Yes, and he certainly is not a local," replied the first man.

Jake tried to move again, but he couldn't. His left shoulder hurt so bad that he couldn't move his arm or hand. His head was throbbing too, but Jake decided that his immediate problem was to be able to think. He struggled to clear his dulled his senses and he finally realized that the men were talking about him. He should be dead. He opened his eyes but he could not focus. His head was swimming and everything was a blur.

Only after several minutes did his senses begin to clear a little and he began to understand that the second person who spoke was talking about him. The man was apparently saying that Jake was one of Burke's men.

Jake needed to clear the air and he tried to raise his head but fell back as he asked, "Where am I?"

A female voice spoke softly, "Just lay back, you are at the Boxed S Sterling Ranch".

He tried to speak again but she said, "You have been shot in the shoulder, and you have a nasty gash on your head and several bruised ribs. You need to lie still; you can tell us your story later." She spoke to the others in the room, "If he is one of Burke's men, who shot him and left him for dead?"

"Well," the last voice said, "I guess that it wouldn't make much sense for him to be one of Burke's men and get shot unless he had a falling out with the Burkes."

She spoke again, "Let's just do the "unless" part later. You men clear out. He needs his rest and besides, he is not going to tell you anything for a while anyway. Sam, have one of the men go for Doc Gray."

Jake heard mumbling from two or three men but he could not make out what they were saying. He went to sleep in spite of his need to find out more.

Some time later Jake woke and became aware of

a perfume fragrance and then saw a beautiful, young lady standing in the doorway. It was difficult to look away, but he did and finally looked around the room. He noticed through the window that it was getting dark. His first reaction was that he had to have been here for several hours or maybe even days. He was still trying to get his bearings when his thoughts were interrupted by the gentle voice of the lady. "You are finally awake. I was beginning to think that you were going to sleep through the night," she said.

He started, "Where am I, how did I get here and what time is it?"

"Whoa now, hold on for a minute. You asked me that question before but you probably do not remember. My name is Rachael Sterling, and my father owns this ranch," she said. "You need to rest. Just wait for a minute and I will get you something to eat. I have some soup that will help you get your strength back. We can talk later."

She quickly left the room and Jake had a chance to really look at his surroundings. He was in a bedroom that appeared to have been occupied by a male at some point. A chair, a table, a wash basin and a lamp were the only items in the room other than the bed. Curtains were hung on the window but they were not fancy curtains.

He was covered by a blanket but lay clothed on the bed except for his shirt and boots. He reached for his gun belt but it was nowhere to be found. He looked around again but did not see the rifle, the shotgun or the 45. The movement caused his head to throb and instinctively he reached his hand to his head. He felt a bandage and he noticed blood on his hand when he brought it down. Apparently, the blood had been seeping through the bandage.

The woman came back with a steamy bowl of soup, a chunk of bread and a cup of black coffee. She placed it on the table and moved the table closer to the bed. "Can you eat by yourself?" she asked.

He attempted to sit up but the pain was unbearable. He decided that he was not going to be able to sit up or eat, and said, "I . . . I don't think so."

She said, "That's okay, I will feed you and then you can rest for awhile, and you'll feel better in the morning." She propped up his head with a pillow and he could feel her nearness and smell the scent of perfume in spite of his throbbing head.

She dipped a spoon in the bowl and brought the soup up to his lips. He remembered that he had not eaten for at least several hours and that he was famished. The soup was hot but felt good as it went down his throat. Soon the soup and the coffee were gone and Rachael Sterling went about putting a new bandage on his head. She had a gentle touch and Jake was almost sorry when she finished.

When she stood to leave the room, Jake stopped her.

"Wait," he said, "you have not told me who you are and where I am and how I got here."

"I told you before that you are at the Sterling Ranch and my name is Rachael, Rachael Sterling," she replied. "Now go back to sleep and you will feel better when you wake up. We can talk in the morning."

"Wait, Miss Sterling, where are my gun and boots?" Jake asked.

"Mr. ah ..."

Jake interrupted, "Call me Jake," he muttered.

"Well, Jake, you will have to wait for your guns until we find out who you are and how you happened to be on the road to the Sterling Ranch," she replied. "Besides," she added, "I don't think that they will be of much use to you tonight." With that she turned and quickly left the room.

Jake was concerned about his guns, but he was in no shape to argue. Finally, he dozed off with the memory of Rachael Sterling and the vanishing perfume. He spent the next several hours in fitful sleep.

When he awoke the sun was streaming in the window and Jake reasoned that it must be past seven. With difficulty, he swung his legs off the bed and sat up. The excruciating pain caused him to become nauseated, and he groaned out loud.

Just as if on cue, the door opened and Rachael walked in. "You may want to rest some more before you try moving around. The gash in your head is deep and you have lost a lot of blood from the gash and the gunshot in your left shoulder. If you move too much you may start bleeding again," she said.

He moved his right hand to his bandaged shoulder and asked, "Is this your handiwork?"

"Oh no, when I saw how serious it was I sent Sam to town for Doc Gray. He is a fine doctor and he does not talk very much, so your location will be safe for a short while," she answered. "The doctor just asked me to change the bandage after the bleeding stopped."

"Thank you and I will be sure to thank the Doc when I get back to town."

"You are in no shape to be going anywhere, especially town. The doctor says that you should stay in bed for several days."

He ignored her last comment and asked, "How long have I been here?"

"I guess that it has been about twenty-four hours since we found you," she replied, and added, "Now lie back down." He obeyed because it was too painful not to.

She looked at Jake and asked, "This ranch is off the beaten path. How did you happen to be on the Sterling Ranch Road? Do you know who shot you?"

"You are moving too fast for me," he replied. "I was leaving Burkeville and stopped to eat breakfast at the café. I picked up some supplies at the general store, picked up my horse and rode out of town. I am not sure what happened, but I remember seeing dust in the distance and I remember thinking that it must have been a wagon from the Sterling Ranch. I headed that way, and at that point I felt a pain in my shoulder and realized that I was falling off my horse. I struggled to stay in the saddle but my horse reared, and I lost my grip. I do not remember hitting the ground so I may have lost consciousness before I hit."

"Well, the dust that you saw was Sam and me in the buckboard. Sam, one of our ranch hands, was taking me into town to buy supplies," she explained. "We heard a shot and we came around the curve and saw your horse and you lying on the ground," she continued. "A rider was on the ridge, and when he saw us he turned and rode away as fast as he could. It appears that when you took a bullet in the shoulder you hit your head on a rock when you fell. The gash is deep and may require another visit to the doctor. Sam and I got you into the buckboard and brought you here," she finished.

"Well, I have no recollection between the time I started falling and when I woke up in this bed," he said. "However, I do have a good notion about what happened. I had a run-in with Burke and some of his men in town yesterday," he reported. "By the way, I heard men saying that I was a Burke man, but I was not able to comprehend all of the conversation."

"All of the new men that ride into Burkeville are

brought in by the Burke Ranch. If they are not brought in they soon are hired by the ranch. So the men just assumed that you were employed by the Burke Ranch," she replied. "And I gather from your conversation that you must be the man that killed Sonny Burke yesterday!" she exclaimed.

"How did you find out?"

"News travels faster than you think around Burkeville."

"Apparently so, yes, I am the same man but it was not something that I planned to do. I didn't even know the man, but he tried to run me out of town. I was just not ready to leave, and he forced my hand."

"Sonny didn't need a reason to be a bully," she replied.

"That's what I heard." Jake explained the events of the last two days and even told her about Johnny and her suggestion that he might want to leave town by the Sterling Ranch rather than the main road.

She agreed that Johnny was correct in her assessment but she suggested that someone probably ambushed him after following him yesterday morning.

Jake remembered the man that had ducked into the alley just before he rode out, but he decided not to say anything about it to Miss Sterling.

"You can stay here for a while, but certainly Burke's men will find you and try to finish the job if you are not careful," she said. "Also, we only have three men on the ranch plus Dad and me, and Dad is in Jones Crossing trying to hire cowhands. Most of ours have been scared off by the threats from the Burkes. The ones that are still here have been around a long time but none of them can use a gun very well," she explained.

"I am going to take your advice and be as careful as I can," Jake replied, "and I will leave as soon as possible, I don't want to cause any problems for you folks."

Rachael turned to go. "I have some work to do," she said, "and I would suggest that you get some rest, so you can get well enough to travel."

Thoughts tumbled through Jake's mind. He realized that it would only be a matter of time before Burke would find out where he was. He was in a tough spot, but he had been in tough spots many times before. He was mulling over his situation and at the same time he was thinking about the two beautiful women that he had met over the past two days. The first of these, Sarah, had taken a disliking to him almost immediately. Then he remembered when Rachael accidentally brushed against him while raising his head and the warmth of that touch. With those beautiful thoughts in his head he dozed off to sleep.

Six

Jake slept through most of the next day and woke up in the evening. Rachael brought him some more soup and coffee, and he ate heartily. She was still not ready to answer his questions and suggested that he go back to sleep. Although he was feeling some better he was still in no shape to argue with her. He slept fitfully.

He was awakened suddenly by loud voices in the front of the house. It took him a few moments to remember where he was, and then he got up as quickly as he could, considering the pain that he was in. He walked out of the bedroom and looked out of the window. It was daylight, and he had slept the whole night. Jake saw three men armed and mounted in the yard. These were no ordinary cowboys, Jake judged. He did not recognize any of the three but they were obviously not friends of the Sterling Ranch. He did notice that one of them had a sling on his left arm. He thought back to the night in the hotel when he was ambushed and the man he had wounded. He glanced toward the right end of the porch and saw Rachael and an older cowboy standing there. Jake reasoned that he must be one of the men Rachael had mentioned the night before. He was not armed.

Jake was quite sure that the three mounted men belonged to the Burke Ranch and that based upon the conversation they were having, it was not a social call. He looked for his gun and gun belt and found them hanging on the wall, just outside the bedroom. He went back to the bedroom and found his boots under the bed. With much difficulty he slipped on his boots, buckled on his gun belt, and tied down the holster. He then checked to make sure that his Colt 45 was fully loaded, and he slipped it back into the holster. His left arm was in a sling and hurting, but he did not think that it would affect his gun hand.

He quietly walked over to the back door, pulled it open and checked to see if anyone was in the back yard. When he was satisfied that all was clear he slipped outside and hugged the side wall until he could see what was going on in the front yard. The three gunmen were paying attention only to the man and Rachael on the porch. Jake took a couple of steps away from the ranch house and spoke loud enough that the three cowboys were startled as they looked in Jake's direction. "I am quite sure that you all are looking for me," said Jake with an icy tone.

"If you are Harn, damn right we are looking for you," the man in the middle quipped.

"Well, you've found me. What are you going to do now?" asked Jake.

"We are going to kill you and feed your rotten hide to the buzzards," shouted the little man on the left with a sling on his left arm.

"Apparently, you failed once at the hotel."

"I don't know what the hell you are talking about, but you are going to die now."

"How are you going to do it, talk me to death?" quipped Jake.

"Why you . . . ," hollered the little man. His voice trailed off as he went for his gun. Jake shot him once in the chest. The man dropped his gun, fell off his horse and lay in a heap, dead.

"Now, you two gents can be reasonable or you can die with your friend," Jake said as he moved the gun to cover the other two cowboys.

The first man who spoke addressed Jake, "Mister, you have bought yourself a lot of trouble," he said scowling.

"Right now my only concern is whether or not we are going to have any more trouble here," replied Jake.

The speaker stared at Jake for a minute then nodded to his friend saying quickly, "Let's get out of here. We can settle the score later."

"Your friend is one smart hombre," said Jake. He added, "Take the gent on the ground with you and tell Burke to use that spot in Boot Hill that he offered me."

The two men dismounted, picked up their dead companion and slung him over his saddle. They mounted again, turned their horses, rode out of the yard and headed down the road, leading the dead man's horse.

Jake holstered his gun and took a few steps to where the horses had been. He noticed that one of the tracks was made by a horse with a loose shoe, the horse that belonged to the tall gent in the middle. He leaned down to study the shoe track closer, but when he tried to get up lost his balance and went down on one knee. Rachael and the older cowboy with her hurried to his side and helped him onto the porch.

"You should have stayed in bed." she scolded Jake "Now your wound is bleeding again." She looked at the other man and said, "Sam, help him back in the house, and I will fix his bandages."

Sam looked at Jake as he supported him and said, in a heartfelt voice, "I am glad that you came out when you did. I was not sure what those men were going to do."

"Hush, Sam," scolded Rachael. "They were just trying to scare us."

He scowled and shook his head. "Even so," he said, "I am sure glad that he was here. I have never seen a gun as fast as Jake's."

"Stop blabbering and get him in the house," she admonished Sam.

"Yes ma'am," he said, and the two men went inside with Jake leaning on Sam for support. Once in his room he lay down on the bed and Sam looked at him, "You are in trouble with Ms. Sterling, and I just remembered that I have a harness in the barn that needs mending."

"So you are just going to leave me alone."

"Yes, sir. Good luck," said Sam, and he walked out the door.

Rachael returned to the room with a pan of hot water and some fresh bandages. She started working on dressing the wound. Her touch was not very gentle. "In spite of what Sam says, you should have stayed in bed," she scolded him." We could have taken care of this situation without bloodshed."

"Miss Sterling, I know men like the ones Burke hires, and they don't care that you are a woman or that Sam was unarmed. They are paid well and that money is the most important thing to them. The only thing that they understand is the lead from a faster gun," he replied.

"They did not even know for sure that you were in the house. We could have stalled them until my father comes back tomorrow bringing some men with him," she said. "If they know that we have more hands, they are less likely to bother us."

"Miss Sterling, I don't think that your father can hire enough men to hold off the Burkes. The kinds of men you need are very expensive," replied Jake.

"My father can handle the situation," she said.

"Can your father use a gun?" asked Jake.

"Of course my father knows how to use a gun," she

stammered defensively. She completed wrapping the bandage on his head and pulled it a little tighter than necessary just to indicate that she was getting the best of the argument. "Just lay back and rest and I'll try to rustle up something for you to eat," she said as she hurried out of the room.

Jake pondered what she said about her father knowing how to use a gun. She had said the right thing but her voice was not convincing. He was also doubtful that her father was going to be able to hire men at Jones Crossing. He knew that there were three hands on the Sterling ranch. He just met Sam and figured that the other two hired men were like Sam when it came to using a gun. Jake had never been to Jones Crossing but he was sure that everyone in town would know the Burkes or their reputation because of the short distance between the two towns. He decided that the only guns that Mr. Sterling could hire would be gunmen and he did not believe that the Sterling Ranch could afford gunmen even if they wanted them. All of these things were going through his mind when he gradually dozed off to sleep.

Sometime later, Rachael came back with a tray of breakfast. She was in a little better mood than before. She set the tray on the table and said that she would be back with some coffee. Jake watched her as she left the room, and then applied himself to eating the eggs and steak. She had not offered to feed him like last time and even though it was painful, he managed to get his breakfast down. Last night's stew had been good, but the steak and eggs were great. Jake decided that he had been hungry and any food was going to be good, especially under these particular circumstances. Rachael came back shortly with coffee and told Jake that when he finished eating he should stay in bed and get some rest.

"I'll be back to check on you later."

For some reason, Jake wanted her to stay but he didn't say anything. He finished off the steak and coffee, washed his hands and face and undressed for bed. Soon he was sound asleep. He woke up a couple times during he night but went back to sleep and he did not wake up again until sunlight was streaming through the window. Once again, he had slept for almost twenty-four hours.

As he roused himself, he realized that the pain in his head was throbbing much less than the afternoon before. His left shoulder felt some better, though it was stiff and almost useless. He decided that he felt like getting out of bed, and he did. He pulled his trousers and shirt on with difficulty and getting the boots on were downright painful. He washed his face in the water pail, slicked his hair down and entered the kitchen.

A tall, thin, distinguished gentleman was sitting at the table drinking coffee and Rachael was standing at the stove. She heard him come in and greeted him,

"Good morning, Jake. You look some better than yesterday."

The man at the table stood up and Rachael said, "Dad, this is Jake Harn, he was shot down on the road. Sam and I carried him to the ranch. Jake, this is my father, Jim Sterling."

They exchanged greetings and Jake said, "Just call me Jake."

"Well, Jake, I understand that you had an unpleasant run-in with the Burkes," Jim Sterling said. He waited for Jake to reply.

"Actually, I had more than one run in, and as you can see I got the worst of at least one of them," said Jake.

"Judging by the bandage you may be right but most everyone in the territory has had a run in with Burke and most of them fared much worse than you did," Sterling replied.

"Will you two stop jabbering," Rachael interrupted, "and sit down and have some coffee? Mr. Harn, I am not the world's best cook and our ranch cook is now working outside the kitchen because we have lost most of our ranch hands."

"No matter," replied Jake, "I am so hungry I could eat a horse."

"Watch out what you are asking for," laughed Jim.

"If you two are not careful, you may have to cook your own," she replied, turning back to the stove.

Jake sipped his coffee and turned to Jim, "Mr. Sterling, I understand that you spent some time in Jones Crossing," he said.

"Yep, sure did. Was looking for some riders for the ranch, but I had no luck. Everyone is afraid to go up against the Burke ranch. They know that he has his sights on controlling the entire valley and will kill anyone that gets in his way," he explained.

"Where do you stand with Burke?" Jake asked.

"Burke and I have had several run-ins. He's made offers to buy the ranch but I've told him that I have no interest in selling to him or anyone else. Jeff Burke and I go back a long time, and I don't think that he wants to push real hard right now. I don't think that we are in immediate danger because of legal issues, but Burke may very well get tired of waiting," he answered.

"How many major ranchers are still in business in the area," asked Jake.

"There are only four major ranches left in the valley other than the Bar B. There are also a handful of one man operations with a few acres that Burke does not really care about. I suspect that he will get rid of them in due time."

"Have you and the other ranchers ever tried to band together to protect yourselves?" asked Jake.

"We have discussed that topic but none of us have enough men to stand up against the thirty or so seasoned gunmen that Burke has at his ranch. The one-man ranchers are not going to do anything because they are not being threatened. What they don't seem to understand is that once the big ranches fall, Burke will gobble them up quickly. "

Rachael interrupted, "Food is served, you can talk later, and the problems are not going away before you finish eating."

Jim yielded to his high-strung daughter and said, "Jake we had better do what she says before she throws out the food."

"I won't argue with her," said Jake.

Jim Sterling offered a short blessing and the two men began eating like they had not eaten for days. Rachel finished preparing the food and sat down at the table. She ate, but sparingly. Soon the two men were finished and Rachel said, "You two go out on the porch, and I will clean up the dishes."

Jokingly Jim said "I was going to help with the dishes but obviously you do not want my help."

She looked at her father and said "Just the same amount of help you have always provided in the kitchen. Go ahead and leave, it will take less time without your help."

The two men smiled at her and went out to the porch. Jake rolled a cigarette and Jim filled his pipe with tobacco. Soon they were puffing and Jim was gazing toward the small pond a few feet away from the house. The water level was low but there were several small trees around the pond to provide some shade.

Jake interrupted Jim's thoughts and asked, "Has Burke made you a realistic offer for the ranch?"

"It depends upon who decides what is realistic. Burke has made an offer to everyone in the valley, but it is not enough to get out of the valley much less get a new start somewhere else," complained Jim bitterly. "I started this ranch nigh on twenty-five years ago when Melissa and I got married," he added, "and she is buried in the plot just beyond those trees. The two of us planted small twigs that have grown to what you see now." He spoke with a tear in his eye. "We put a lot of work and sweat in the ranch and it looks like we are going to lose the whole thing."

Jake looked at Jim and realized that he was seriously concerned about losing everything he had worked for so long. He spoke to Jim, "I am not much good right now as a cowhand, but I would like to stay around a few days if it will not cause you too much trouble."

Jim replied, "Stay as long as you like. Trouble will come whether or not you are here."

"Do you have a plan?" asked Jake.

"The only plan that I had was to try and hire more men, but that didn't work. I can't afford to import gunmen and regular cow hands are afraid to hire on. "

Jake looked at Jim and said, "I would like to look around the ranch if you don't mind. I have some experience as a cowhand. I might be able to earn my keep."

Jim replied, "I appreciate that, but you are only one man and my other men will not be much help. They are old and none of the three can use a gun very well. Besides, I really don't want them to get hurt."

"I will try not to do anything that will get anyone killed, including me." He turned to go and then stopped and asked, "By the way Jim, how about the sheriff?"

"Ben Mason has been sheriff for some ten years, and he is a good man, but he cannot buck Burke and his men. I think that he is sympathetic to us, but Burke would just as soon kill the sheriff as anyone else," answered Jim.

"What about the other ranchers?" asked Jake.

"As I said earlier, there are only four of them, and they are as bad off as we are. Only a few hands each and, far as I know, none of them can handle a gun against Burke's men."

"Are there men in town that you could count on in case of an emergency?" asked Jake.

"When it comes to gun play, I can't think of anyone that would back the Sterling Ranch or anyone else against the Burkes," replied Jim.

Jake rose, and carefully extinguished his cigarette. "I am going to try and ride a little if I can get my horse saddled, see you later," he said.

"I'll have Sam saddle your horse."

"Thanks but I can do it myself. "

"Okay, but you be very careful where you ride. Burke's men are not choosey about whose land they ride on," warned Jim. Then he continued, "Jake, my daughter told me about the problem with the three men, and I thank you for helping her."

"I will be careful but I was the reason those men were here so it was my duty to interfere."

"Just the same, I don't know all of Burke's men but it is no doubt that they were looking for you. Again, I appreciate your help but I don't want your blood on my hands."

"Thanks for the warning and I appreciate your concern."

Jake left the house through the kitchen, nodding to Rachael as he went out the door.

Rachael stared after him a moment and tried to decide what attracted her to him. She found no quick answer, so she went back to work.

Seven

The two men that Jake ran off the Sterling Ranch were not only mad about their treatment by Jake but they were also concerned about having to face Burke. Jeff Burke paid good wages for gunmen, and he expected results. The two discussed the situation and what they were going to tell Burke, but no good ideas came to them.

The taller of the two said, "Ike, I'll be dammed if I was going to drag my gun after I saw Harn shoot Diego. That would have been suicide."

"Dave, I understand that, but the question is will Burke understand?" replied Ike.

The two of them rode into the Burke ranch and tied their horses at the rail. They had left the body of Diego in town at the undertakers and brought his horse back to the ranch. They looked at each other as they prepared to go inside and face Burke.

The one called Dave knocked on the door and Burke hollered, "Come in." The two walked into the office and found Burke sitting at his large wooden desk.

Burke looked at Dave Egan for a few moments waiting for him to speak. When he didn't, he asked, "Where is Diego?"

Dave Egan, the spokesman for the two men, answered Burke hesitantly, "Well, Diego got himself killed."

Burke stared at the man and asked sarcastically, "And just who killed him?"

"Uh --oh, well, Harn killed him," responded Egan.

"I sent out three men to do a job and only two came back. You had better have a good explanation."

"Boss, we went to the Sterling Ranch like you said and while we were talking to the girl and old Sam, Harn got the drop on us," said Ike.

"Diego is dead and you two are here without Harn or his body?" shouted Burke.

"We dropped Diego's body off in town but, Boss, Harn surprised us, and besides he is the fastest man I have ever seen with a gun," responded Egan.

Burke, getting angrier by the minute said, "You fool, I am talking about Harn's body, I don't give a damn about Diego's body."

Ike piped up, "Diego is, or was, fast, but Harn shot him before he could get off a shot and Harn only needed one shot."

"And pray tell me what the hell were the two of you doing while Harn gunned down Diego?" shouted Burke even louder than before.

"Well, Boss, he was so fast that we didn't have a chance . . . ."

"Egan, you had a chance to kill him before with a

rifle but you muffed that job too, didn't you?"

"But, Boss, I . . ."

"Never mind," interrupted Burke. "Get Roddy in here and you two get out of my sight," he added. The two men turned and walked out of the office without another word.

A few minutes later, the Bar B foreman knocked on the door and walked into Burke's office, "Want to see me, Boss?" he asked.

"Yes, Roddy, I guess you heard that the three men we sent to find Harn came back short a man that Harn killed," he said.

"Yep, I heard that, and I understand that this Harn is mighty quick with a gun," responded Roddy.

"Never mind that, I have a plan to take care of Mr. Harn," Burke answered. "I want you to send a telegram to Dodge City and request the services of a gun fighter."

"Do you have someone in mind?" asked the foreman.

"Yes, Jack Slade, I understand that he is the best in these parts."

"But Boss, I have heard of Slade and, I understand that he is good but we don't need an outside gun, we have plenty here," he replied.

"Apparently none of them are good enough," snarled Burke. "Besides, an outsider would draw less suspicion."

"Why do we care about suspicion? We control most of the valley, and we plan to control all of it. No one can stop us. Harn is only one man. He might be fast, but we have thirty guns," he replied.

"Use your head. We have kept the sheriff neutral in our plans, and we want to continue to do so to ensure that he does not try to call in the federal marshals," Burke explained.

"Why not just kill Mason, and we won't have to worry about it?" asked Roddy.

"Sometimes I wonder what I am paying you for. If the sheriff is killed it's sure to cause an investigation. That's the problem around here, no one thinks." Burke wrote some information on a piece of paper and handed it to Roddy. "I trust you with this information, and I do not want anyone else to know, do you understand?"

"Sure, Boss, I'll leave for town right away," replied Roddy. "I want to visit someone in town so I will probably stay over."

"I know who you are visiting and remember, no one, including her, is to know about the telegram even though it does not name Harn," cautioned Burke.

"I'll be careful," said Roddy. He put the paper in his shirt pocket and left the room. He headed for the bunkhouse to get his things. Fortunately, none of the other hands were there so that eliminated the necessity of explaining his trip. He changed his shirt, combed his hair and headed for the barn. He reasoned that it was early enough to get to town before dark and maybe have time for a drink or two at the saloon. He saddled his horse and headed out.

Roddy spent some time at the telegraph office getting the telegram sent, before heading to the café. He ate sparingly, paid for his meal and headed for the saloon. When he got there he was surprised to see Dave Egan and Ike Winters drinking at the bar.

The foreman looked at the pair and said, "The boss is mighty sore at both of you."

"We know, that's why we decided to lay low for a spell," replied Egan.

"That's probably a good thing to do. You two ride back to the ranch, but stay clear of the boss. I'll be riding out early in the morning."

"Okay by us, but why are you here tonight?" asked Egan.

"Aw, the boss wanted me to run an errand. Drink up and get on back to the ranch."

"Roddy, I still want another crack at Harn," said Egan.

"Take my advice and leave him alone before you get killed. The boss has a plan to take care of Harn," replied the foreman. "I have some business in town. I'll be back at the ranch tomorrow."

Egan laughed and said, "We know what your business is."

"Never mind your jokes, just get on back to the ranch." The two men nodded to the big foreman and headed for the door.

Eight

After leaving the Sterling Ranch, Jake, knowing that the pain from his injuries would limit his time in the saddle, decided to cover as much land as he could before heading back to the ranch. He was not sure what he was looking for, but he wanted to get a better picture of the Sterling Ranch. He decided to locate as many water holes that he could, since a good supply of water was high on the priority list for any ranch.

He left the path he was on and rode off into a wash. Several yards ahead he found water along with tracks of a couple of hundred cows. The water hole was very small, and it was strange that that so many cows would be bunched so closely. He dismounted and walked up a small bank. There he saw shod horse tracks. It now became clear that the cows had been held there for a short time before moving them out.

When he examined the horse tracks he noticed that one of them was familiar, very much like the one he had seen at the Sterling ranch. Jake followed the tracks for a while and saw that they disappeared into some thick brush.

He rode to the entrance of a partially-hidden road

and carefully continued through the thick underbrush until he reached a larger spring. He dismounted and examined the many tracks that surrounded the water hole. He noticed that some of the tracks were made by deer and other wild animals but most were made by cattle and horses. He was curious about the track that matched the one from the Sterling Ranch. It appeared to be made by a horse with a warped shoe, noticeably different from the others. Jake made a mental note to try and find out the name of the owner of that horse.

Jake filled up his canteen, made sure that Muddy had drunk his fill from the waterhole and rode on. He was careful to avoid any areas where he could be ambushed. He had been riding for an hour or so when he came upon an opening that looked out over a large ravine. Jake sat still for several minutes and gazed out over the beautiful landscape and the hundreds of cattle grazing in the valley.

He was not exactly sure whose property he was on, but he was curious about the large number of cattle seeming to be hidden away from other cattle. He took his binoculars from his saddle bag and scanned the entire area. When his gaze reached the far side of the ravine his eyes settled on a small clump of trees and a camp site where two cowboys were drinking coffee at a camp fire and two horses were grazing close by, near a small spring.

Jake wanted to get a look at the brands on the cattle

but he didn't want to be seen. He tied Muddy to a bush in the thicket and walked toward the side of the ravine farthest from the camp. It gave him enough cover to keep from being seen until he got into the open. The only cover consisted of two dead logs only a few feet from the thicket. He took off his hat and gun belt and left them in the thicket. He then took his 45 and stuffed it in his trousers. He slung the binoculars over his neck and started crawling toward the logs.

The logs were only fifty or so feet away and he reached them easily. He was able to see some of the brands. To his surprise some of the cattle were from the Sterling Ranch. With the help of the binoculars he was also able to identify two other brands. One was Double C and the other was Rocking J. He did not recognize the brands but he thought it peculiar that he did not see any Bar B stock.

By the looks of things, the cattle had been rustled and were being held here. Most likely they would be held until the heat was off then sold. Again, he thought, why no Bar B stock, unless…? The "unless" led Jake to consider the possibility that the Bar B could be behind the rustling. He recalled the conversation with Jim Sterling about the Bar B wanting control of the valley and certainly one way to get it would be to steal the cattle so that the few remaining ranchers could not sell enough stock to pay their mortgages. He decided that this situation was worth looking into later.

Jake back-tracked to his horse, mounted and rode back toward the Sterling Ranch. The sun was going down, and he realized that he had been gone most all day. He also realized that he was hungry and in pain. His thoughts wandered to Rachael Sterling. She was a wonderfully caring woman, and he would be very lucky to make a connection with her. But, deep down he couldn't help thinking about Sarah Garnett. Sarah was beautiful, refined, and obviously educated. On the other hand Rachael was pretty but more practical—through and through a rancher's daughter.

As he rode on, he admonished himself. Why am I thinking about either of these women? Sarah Garnett obviously hates me, and Rachael Sterling and her father could very well be leaving the valley unless someone can stop Burke. He touched his spurs to Muddy's flanks, who responded quickly. A short time later he rode into the corral at the Sterling Ranch.

Rachael greeted him on the front porch and asked, "Where have you been, Jake Harn? You are not well enough to be riding that long."

"Are you scolding me?" asked Jake.

"You're darn right I am," she replied. "I was worried that something might have happened to you."

"Something probably will happen to me if I don't get some grub," he said to her with a grin.

"Oh. . . you . . . . You make me so mad," and she swiftly turned and headed back into the house. Jake followed her into the kitchen.

"Sit down at the table and I will get you something to eat," she grumbled.

Jake threw his hat in the corner and pulled up a chair at the table. "Where is your father?" he asked Rachael.

"He and the other hands are trying to round up some strays that have wandered off," she replied.

He thought about not telling her what he discovered but decided that she had a right to know. "Has your father mentioned anything about losing any cattle lately?" he asked.

"Why no," she replied, "but again, we do not have enough men to keep watch on our livestock." Then she added, "Why do you ask?"

Just as Jake was about to explain, they heard horses coming in. "That'll be dad now." A short time later Jim Sterling walked in the door.

"Dad, I was just about to put some food on the table. Wash up and sit down," said Rachael.

"Thanks, Daughter, and howdy, Jake," answered Jim. "It has been a long day and not much was accomplished," he added.

"How so?" asked Jake.

"Well, we spent hours combing the south range and we were only able to locate a couple hundred cows," explained the rancher.

"I may be able to shed some light on your problem,"

said Jake.

Rachael set the hot food and coffee down and suggested that they eat before it got cold. Neither of the two men needed any further encouragement because both were extremely hungry. They dug in, and Jake waited to explain what he had seen until they finished the meal and sat back to enjoy the refilled coffee.

Jake took the next several minutes to tell what he had discovered about the cattle and the men that were apparently holding the herd in the valley. When he finished, he asked the rancher about all of the brands in the valley and if there was a legitimate reason why the brands were bunched up together.

Jim seemed surprised and answered, "None that I am aware of. We tried to get together with some of the smaller ranches to round up the stock, but we were not very successful because none of the ranchers could provide enough men to move or hold the cattle," replied the rancher.

"In light of what I have seen, I think that later on I am going to pay a visit to the other ranchers and find out about their cattle. When they realize that their cows have been rustled they may decide that they have no choice but to band together," said Jake.

"Why don't we just take the boys and cut out our stock and drive them back on to Sterling property?" asked Jim.

"Too risky with the few men you have. We'll have to

wait for a better opportunity," replied Jake.

"Well, just be very careful that you stay out of range of the Burke's gunmen," Jim cautioned.

"Thanks for the warning." Jake walked to the stove and asked for a refill for his coffee.

Rachael answered, "Sit down, and I will get it for you."

"I appreciate your hospitality, Ma'am."

"Do you consider yourself a southern gentleman," she asked with a smile.

"Absolutely, born and raised," he responded.

She put a cup of coffee in front of him and then turned serious and asked, "Why are you risking your neck to help us? You could just ride out and avoid Burke. No one would blame you for leaving."

"Getting out of the territory may not be that easy. Remember Burke has vowed to kill me. Besides you took me in when I needed help and I owe you something, and I don't like to be forced to do anything that I don't want to do. You say that no one would blame me. Well, I would blame myself if I rode out."

"How did you happen to ride into Burkeville?" she asked.

"I guess that I am just lucky, or unlucky. I had no real place to go, and I happened to ride in this direction."

"Where is your home?" she asked.

"I was born and raised in Georgia several miles

south of Savannah. My family owned a large plantation and before the War Between the States we raised
and shipped cotton to the mills in Savannah."

"Why did you leave?"

"I was on the wrong side of the conflict."

"How did you get involved in the war?"

"You ask a lot of questions from a stranger that you
hardly know," he said with a smile.

"Well, if you don't want to tell me . . ." her voiced
trailed off as she turned her back to him.

He took a sip of the coffee and said, "I don't really
mind. I was 22 when the war broke out and I, along
with many others, heard the call to defend our honor.
We endured great hardship and when it was over the
South was in shambles."

"What did you do after the war?" she asked.

"I went back home and saw lots of devastation
along the way, but I had no real idea how bad it was until I got back to Savannah. Savannah itself was spared,
but the farms and plantations in the countryside were
destroyed. When the war was over, my family had
lost everything from the land to buildings and the live
stock. All of it courtesy of Yankee General Sherman
and his scorched earth policy."

"You couldn't get the land back? How about the local law?" she asked.

"You must understand the situation in the old Con-
federacy. The south is a conquered land and to the vic-

tors go the spoils—including our family plantation," he replied bitterly.

"Well, what happened to your folks?"

"Mom and Dad moved into a house in Savannah, and he took a job offered by one of his former business associates. My only sister got married and moved to Charleston, South Carolina."

Rachael put her hand on Jake's shoulder and said, "That must have been just awful."

"I have to admit that it caused me to see more of the country than I expected," he replied with a forced grin.

"I am sure that your folks took it hard when you left," she said.

"The last time I spoke to my father, he said, "Jake, we are not welcome in our own community, and you are young enough to start over. The best thing that you can do is head west and build a new life for yourself and your future family."

"And you just took off and left."

"Well, after looking at my options, which were slim, I decided to heed his advice. I had a little money left from my army days, so I headed west. I really had no idea where I was going, but I thought about Colorado territory or maybe even California. That was over six years ago and a lot of water has flowed under the bridge since then."

He stood up. "Time to go," he said.

"What are you planning to do tomorrow?" she asked.

"I'm not real sure, but there has to be something that can be done," he answered.

"Please be careful," she said with concern in her voice.

"What's the matter, are you going to miss me when I'm gone?"

"Can't you ever be serious?" she asked.

"Maybe tomorrow," he winked at Rachael and headed for the bunk house.

Rachael finished up in the kitchen and decided to read for a while. She tried to read but she couldn't concentrate on her book. She undressed, lay down and tried to go to sleep but she kept thinking about Jake Harn. She tried to tell herself that he was protecting himself and that he was not really interested in her. And she definitely was not interested in him. Definitely...

But there was something strange about him, strange and exciting. She went to sleep remembering how Jake Harn moved and talked, and the way that he looked at her. She got goose bumps just thinking about him.

Nine

The next morning Jake dressed and rode into town. He knew that Burke had a loyal following in the area. He thought that many of the other townspeople might simply be afraid to act differently. He reasoned that this group of people if they banded together might be able to break Burke's strangle-hold on the town. It's possible that the Burkes might not have as much power as some folks thought, he told himself. He knew that the group would need a leader, and he suspected that it would have to be him. Then he asked himself if this was something that he really wanted to get involved in. Last night Rachael had asked him the same question, and he had responded readily with an all-too-noble answer. However, that noble answer may have come from the heart rather than the head. Whatever he decided to do, he knew that the answers were not going to come easy.

As he rode he pondered the Sterling Ranch situation. It would be easier for him to just ride out of the territory and forget about the people in Burkeville. Rachael had even said so herself. On the other hand, there were a lot of very good people and some had helped him out a great deal. Jim Sterling was a decent person and his daughter was a wonderful and beautiful young woman. Jake thought that he could do a lot worse than hooking up with Rachael, but then he dismissed the thought quickly. Rachael was too young and besides she was probably being nice to him just because he was injured.

Jake himself had brought about some of the Sterling's problems by shooting a Burke man at the ranch. Jake was going to take the problem to the sheriff. Sterling did not believe that they would get much help from the sheriff, but he wanted to explore all avenues. Jake knew that the sheriff was not fond of him because of his failure to cooperate after the shooting, but hadn't Sterling said that the sheriff was basically a good man? It was possible that he could be convinced to help out.

Jake's thoughts turned to the other ranchers. The small local ranchers only had a few cowhands and apparently none of them were gunmen. Jake was not normally in favor of hiring gunmen but now he was convinced that the valley and the Sterling Ranch were in need of them. Jake did not consider himself a gunman but he had spent several years in the army and become proficient with pistols, rifles and shotguns. His use of a hand gun and the fast draw and shoot idea only came after he got out of the army. He was born and raised on a plantation where problems were not resolved by drawing from the hip and shooting the adversary.

After Jake was mustered out of the army, he spent

a couple of months in Savannah visiting his parents and looking for a job. With the plantation gone, he had some money from the army but it would not last long without a job. His dad suggested that Jake go west, and eventually he took a train from Savannah, Georgia to Independence, Missouri and joined a wagon train. Jake had only been on the wagon train a few weeks when he killed his first man after being discharged from the army. This killing came about because Jake was carrying a pistol in his belt when an ex-Yankee soldier began harassing him for being a confederate soldier. He attempted to ignore the man but when his adversary drew a gun, Jake killed him.

The wagon master was sympathetic toward Jake but he still asked him to leave the train to keep peace with the other travelers. Before Jake left the wagon train the wagon master gave Jake some advice, "Jake, you have a temper, and you carry a gun. My advice is that you get rid of the gun or become faster drawing that thing."

Jake did not want to get rid of the gun so he took the wagon master's advice and began practicing his fast draw. He was very good at hitting what he aimed at, and now, after hours and hours of practice, he could both draw quickly and hit his target.

When he left the wagon train he drifted for a while and found odd jobs at ranches. The jobs gave him time to continue to practice with his pistol and learn as much as he could about ranching. For a while he even worked as a ranch foreman.

Jake drifted further west. For a time he served as deputy marshal in Baxter Springs, Kansas. That is where he had to shoot his second man, and decided at that time that he did not really want to be a lawman. The second killing happened during an attempted bank robbery and shootout. Soon after the killing, Jake quit his job, moved on, and two weeks later he rode into Burkeville and ran into Sonny Burke.

He was still in deep thought when he reached the outskirts of Burkeville. He decided to play it safe and ride into town without being noticed. Jake was sure that Burke had men posted around the town and he didn't want them to see him before he wanted them to. He came in from the north and tied Muddy in a clump of trees just outside of town. He reached Main Street near the café, where he decided to get some food and see if he could get any information about the Burkes that might be helpful to the Sterling Ranch. There were no patrons in the café, so Jake walked in, took a seat in the corner, and waited for the waitress to appear.

Soon afterward Johnny came out of the kitchen and stared at Jake. "I heard that someone shot at you a few days ago," she said.

"Well you heard right, Johnny, but apparently the shooter had poor aim," he explained with a humorous smile.

"How many times does it take to make you understand that you are in trouble? Why are you back in town when someone is trying to kill you?" she asked.

"Looking for information," he said. "But first I need some food, if you have any." He looked around the room and said, "The information can wait."

She stared at Jake for a full minute before walking away toward the kitchen. She returned a short time later with ham, eggs, bread and coffee. "Eat up, if you are so doggone hungry," she said.

"Thank you, Ma'am," Jake replied with a smile.

"And don't call me Ma'am," she answered, "My name is Johnny."

She walked back to the kitchen, and Jake began hungrily eating. He had finished and was drinking the coffee when she came back and poured another cup.

"Say, Johnny, how much do you know about the sheriff, Ben Mason?" he asked.

"I thought that you had an argument with the sheriff in the saloon. Why would you want to know about him?" she asked.

"I understand that he is a reasonable feller, and he may be able to work with me in spite of the misunderstanding," he explained.

She thought a moment and said, "Ben is a good man and a good sheriff, but I believe that he realizes that he cannot buck the Burke Ranch so he just decided to take care of himself," she replied.

"What do you think about the chances that the sheriff would back the ranchers with a battle against Burke?" he asked.

"It probably would depend on how many other people you can count on," she answered. "I'm sure that he would not do anything against Burke without lots of help."

"Does he have any deputies?"

"I don't believe that he has had any for some time. I believe that he would be willing to hire one but I am not sure that he could find anyone that would agree to take the job."

"How much do you know about the other ranchers?" he asked.

"Several of the ranchers have sold out to Burke for a very low price and left the county," she replied. "Only four other major ranchers including Burke and Sterling are left," she added.

"That's all?"

"Well, there are a handful of small ranches that are one man operations."

"Any chance that any of the ranchers other than Sterling would make a fight against Burke?" asked Jake.

"The smaller ranchers have not been bothered by Burke yet so it is doubtful that they would agree to participate. Brad Jason of the Rocking J is a hot head, and he may be persuaded if he thinks that he could get help but he only has two or three men and none of them are gunmen," she answered.

"How about the other two?" he prodded.

"Trent Cochran owns the Double C Ranch, he is a reasonable man. He would have to be convinced that they could win. I wouldn't waste your time with the others," she suggested.

"Anyone else other than the ranchers that could be depended upon in a pinch?"

"If I were you I wouldn't count on anyone around here," she said.

"That's not what I wanted to hear but much obliged," said Jake as he left some money on the table and headed for the door.

"Mister, you be careful nosing around, someone may take exception."

"I know, you can't afford to lose any good customers," he shouted back.

"Who said that you're a good customer?" she replied with a laugh.

Jake walked along the buildings being careful to stay in the shadows as he walked from the café to the sheriff's office. He looked in the window and saw that Ben Mason was setting at his desk working on paperwork. Jake opened the door and walked in. The startled sheriff looked up.

"Evenin', Sheriff," drawled Jake.

"Evenin', Harn. What brings you here?" he asked wryly.

"Sheriff, I'm sure that you heard about someone taking pot-shots at me a few days ago."

"Harn, everybody in town knows that you were shot but no one knows who did it, or can prove it," replied the sheriff.

"Sheriff, I think that you and everyone else in town know that I was shot by one of Burke's men or even Burke himself," retorted Jake disgustedly.

The sheriff sighed, "Let's say that you are correct. What can I or you, do about it? Everyone that does not work for Burke and some that do are too scared to do or say anything about him or what goes on."

"Where do you fit in, Sheriff?" Jake asked.

The sheriff's face became red and his anger began building. "Look, Harn, I have no deputies and Burke has more than thirty gunmen, what would you have me do?" he asked.

"How about sending for federal marshals?" replied Jake.

"If Burke had any inkling that I was sending for anyone, he would kill me and anyone else that was involved. Burke plans to own this whole county and there is very little that you or I or anyone else can do about it," he shrugged.

"So we just wait and let it happen?" Jake asked.

The Sheriff opened the drawer of the desk and took out a deputy's badge. "Harn, I have several badges and the authorization to pay for deputies. We could start by having you and others put on a badge like this," he replied. "And before you say anything else, I just happen to know that you worked as a deputy in the past."

"I see you've done some checking," Jake responded.

"That is normal procedure when we have a high profile gent such as yourself ride into town," the sheriff replied.

"Sheriff, I am not really interested in wearing a badge, but I would be willing to participate. My question is can we count on you when the time comes?" said Jake.

"Again, I'm one man. I can't promise you much help. Besides, what could I do?"

"Well, first of all, how about providing some information."

"Such as?"

"Such as how much do you know about the killing in Jones Crossing that involved Sonny Burke?"

"Not much for sure but I do know Sheriff Tom Benson. I had a conversation with him not long after it happened and his story is that he and his deputy arrested Sonny and a day or two later the judge let him go."

"Have any idea why?"

"I really don't know the judge and there is no evidence to prove it, but there was talk that the release had something to do with Jeff Burke."

"Money?"

"Don't think so, the judge has money, but the talk centered on something from his past in New Orleans, I believe, where he came from."

"Much obliged," said Jake.

"You said the first thing, what is the second thing?" asked the sheriff.

"You know any men around town that could be persuaded to work with me at the Sterling Ranch?"

The sheriff scratched his chin and thought for a moment. "That would be hard to say. The only prospects that I can think of are the three gents that were in the saloon when you had the altercation with Sonny Burke."

"You know their names?"

"Yeah, uh...Rusty Yates, Billy Cannon and Steve Underwood."

"Cowhands?"

"Very good at what they do, but they are not gun hands."

"Cowhands will do for now, thanks, Sheriff."

"You mentioned something else?"

"Yeah, but hopefully I will be able to explain it later," said Jake

"Let me know what you are up to, and I would suggest that you be very careful. Lots of people would shoot you to please Burke and collect the reward," replied the sheriff.

"Reward?"

"The word on the street is $500 dead. So be careful who you associate with."

"I plan to be very careful and thanks for your help," replied Jake as he turned to go.

"By the way, Harn, I have a message for you. Do you know a gent named L. Q. Cranbrook?"

Jake sighed and replied, "I'm sorry to say, I do."

The sheriff handed the telegram to Jake.

"Have a habit of reading other people's mail, Sheriff?" asked Jake.

"Just want to know what's going on in my town."

"I assume you can tell me what the telegram says?" asked Jake.

"Do you know a gent name Slade?"

"Sorry to say I'm acquainted with him, too."

"Jack Slade is what it says. The telegram says that Jack Slade has been hired to kill someone in Burkeville, and obviously Mr. Cranbrook believes it's you."

Jake took the telegram and studied it for a few moments and put it back in the envelope. He puzzled at the message but had no immediate answer. He nodded to the sheriff, put the envelope in his pocket and walked out of the door into the street, and headed for the Trail's End Saloon. Jake came away convinced that Sheriff Ben Mason would help under the right circumstances. He obviously was careful to know what was going on, but smart enough to know he couldn't do much about it.

Jake walked into the saloon and stopped just inside the door. He scanned the room to see if he recognized anyone, but he didn't. He had decided to get a beer before riding back to Brad Jason's ranch. Several men were drinking and playing cards and two men slouched against the bar, eyeing Jake cautiously. Both men were good size with one being of average height and squat, but the other was huge. His shoulders were massive and he had hands like bear paws.

Jake looked away and stepped up to the bar and asked for a beer. The barkeep brought the beer and spoke quietly to Jake, "They were talking about you before you came in. The one on the left is Roddy Spencer, foreman of the Bar B. The other gent is just called Fallon, and he is as tough as can be."

"Much obliged Pat. Glad to know that I am important enough to talk about," replied Jake.

The one called Fallon looked at Jake and demanded, "You Jake Harn?"

"That's what they call me," Jake responded.

The big man looked at the man called Roddy and said, "You know, Boss, I never cared for the name Jake."

The foreman laughed but Jake didn't respond.

Fallon was not accustomed to being ignored. He looked at Jake and said, "And I don't think that I like you either," He raised his voice and began to turn red in the face.

Jake stared at his beer for a moment and responded, "Sorry that you don't like my name or me but, first of all, I don't care whether you like me or not and, second of all, I don't know you and you don't know me."

"I know that you killed Sonny Burke, and that is all I need to know. But I also know that you are causing problems for Mr. Burke, and that's what I care about," continued Fallon.

"Fallon, or whatever your name is, I believe that you have heard it all wrong. Burke and his men are the ones causing the problems, and I am just taking care of myself," replied Jake.

"It doesn't matter, either way you tell it. I'd just suggest you leave town and there won't be no more problems." Now he was shouting at Jake.

"Fallon, I was told by Burke that leaving town was not an option, and now I believe that there is a price on my head. I will tell you and everyone else that I have no intention of leaving town, and I'll deal with any problems that may come along. I am staying until I am ready to leave," said Jake.

"Burke is a friend of mine and he's my boss. He takes care of me so if you are an enemy of Burke, you are my enemy," he continued, "and Burke wants you dead and so do I."

"You sure don't care who your friends are," said Jake wryly. He looked at the Bar B foreman and spoke, "If this is one of your goons, you may want to put him on a tighter leash."

"Who the hell do you think you are, calling me a goon?" bellowed Fallon.

Roddy put his arm in front of Fallon and looked at Jake, "Harn, look at this man. Fallon is not very smart but he pretty much does what he wants to, and I wouldn't hold him back if I could," said the foreman with a broad grin on his face.

It was clear to Jake that the foreman was encouraging Fallon to fight Jake, and it was even clearer that he was getting into a dangerous spot with very few options. A little voice in the back of his mind told him to finish his drink and walk out of the door. That probably made sense, but walking away from a confrontation had never been Jake's way. He could already hear the crowd laughing as he walked out of the room. He thought about his other options and decided they were slim. The only other option was to take his chances with this bear of a man. Jake realized that he had a bad arm and it may not be much use in a fight. His headache had gone away but the injury had not healed.

Jake had a lot of experience using his fists. On the Georgia plantation, boxing was a sport that most of the young men participated in, and Jake was normally the winner in his matches. Unfortunately, none of the young men he boxed looked like Fallon and Jake had never boxed with an injured arm.

He glanced back at the two, and the foreman was

the picture of anticipation. He had seen men battered and nearly killed by Fallon and he was sure that it was going to happen again. Jake moved his attention to Fallon. His first impression was correct, and he may have been even bigger than he had first thought. He was a towering big man with broad shoulders, long arms and big meaty hands. He also noticed that his knuckles bore the scars of many other battles.

Jake decided that the only way to get out of the saloon was through Fallon. "Okay, Fallon, I have things to do, if this is what you want, we may as well get at it," said Jake.

"Harn, if you are smart you can always just walk right out the door, keep going and hope that Burke doesn't catch up with you," said the foreman. "Fallon won't follow you."

"No one ever told me I was smart," retorted Jake.

"Harn, as you can see, I do not carry a gun, I only use these," said Fallon, as he held up his huge hands.

Jake looked at those hands and shuddered before saying, "We can settle this without a gun."

The bartender slid down the bar toward Jake and whispered, "Harn, are you crazy? I am sure that Fallon has killed men with his bare hands, and many were much bigger than you."

Jake looked at the bartender with a determined smile and said, "This is something that I have to do, Pat. Do you think that you can keep the crowd out of it until we get outside?"

The barkeep spoke softly, "I'll do what I can, but how?"

"Do you have a scatter gun behind the bar?"

"I sure do and both barrels are loaded."

"Just be careful, I don't want anyone hurt including me."

"I know how to use this thing. Do you have a plan?"

Jake looked at him and said, "I need to get this fight outside so that I can box and have room to stay away from this big ape."

The bartender whispered, "Well, I might be able to help you with that." He walked down to the end of the bar and quickly pulled out the shotgun. He put the gun to his shoulder and pointed it at the foreman and Fallon. He raised his voice and said, "There will be no problems in here. Take your fight outside, I can't afford the damage."

Roddy looked at the bartender and said, "You know, Pat, the boss will not like you interfering with his business.

"Roddy, I'm just trying to protect my establishment."

Fallon sneered at the bartender and said, "Inside or outside it won't make any difference." He headed for the door and looked at Jake, "Let's not take too long. I'll think that you are yellar." He pointed to Jake and beckoned him outside. Jake nodded at the bartender and followed the big man out the door.

Everyone emptied out of the saloon in anticipation of the fight. Jake thought that if there were bets on the fight, he certainly would not be the favorite. The men jostled each other to find a good view point close around Fallon and Jake. Fallon took off his shirt, showing the size and bulk of his huge frame. Jake followed, taking off his shirt and gun belt and tossed them toward the bartender. Jake was a powerful man, but even in his best days he would not be able to match Fallon's strength. He knew that his best chance was to rely on his boxing skills and stay away from the big man.

Fallon was confident and he tried to rush Jake right away, but Jake circled the big man for a few moments, trying to find an advantage. Fallon took a few wild swings that Jake easily dodged. Apparently, he was not used to missing so he rushed Jake. Jake watched the big man's eyes and anticipated the move. He stepped aside using his speed and hooked a left to the big man's belly and then brought a smashing right into his teeth. The left hand had an effect but the pain from the injury almost caused Jake to black out.

The big man spit blood and snarled at Jake, "A boxer huh? I eat boxers for dinner."

"You are going to have to move faster and talk less if you are going to get close enough," said Jake between clenched teeth.

Fallon moved in again and Jake feinted and hit the big man again with a right hand but he was not quick enough to get away clean. As he was falling back Fallon unleashed a big right hand just missing Jake flush but it had enough steam to rock Jake's head back. Jake shook his head to get rid of the cobwebs and he searched for Fallon. Fallon's face was bloody, but he was still coming. Jake stepped inside again, blocked a big right hand and threw his best right hand and it landed square on the jaw of Fallon.

Fallon stumbled and Jake moved in again and hit him in the mid section causing Fallon to fall to his knees. Before Fallon could get up out of his crouch, Jake brought his knee up into his lowered face with full force. The crack of the knee on Fallon's mouth could be heard by everyone in the audience. The blood flowed freely from his mouth and busted nose.

Fallon put one of his hands on the ground to keep from falling on his bloody face. He stumbled toward the water trough and grabbed the side of it to help raise himself up to his feet.

Fallon looked at Jake and spluttered, "It's not over yet, I'm going to crush you to death."

"Save your breath, Fallon, you are going to have to do better than what you've done so far," replied Jake.

"Hell with you, Harn, I'm also going to crack your skull," shouted Fallon as he moved toward Jake.

Jake said nothing and just waited for Fallon to close

in. He side-stepped and hit him with a hard right on the side of his head but he was not quick enough to dodge the big right hand of Fallon. The blow caught Jake on the left ear, knocking him off balance. He was able to stay upright by holding on to the porch rail. It felt like something was rattling in his head, but he was able to shake it off and stay away from Fallon until he could catch his breath. Fallon was bleeding profusely and he had slowed down his charge. Jake was out of breath and was covered with blood. He didn't know if it was his blood or Fallon's. After getting his breath, Fallon moved in again. Jake was able to avoid the flailing fists and threw a short jab that landed right on the nose of Fallon. He then hit him three more times as fast as he could jab. Fallon was trying to cover up but Jake hit him in the throat, causing Fallon to bend over and grasp for air. Jake, sensing the end, threw a hammer from another right hand, connecting in the kidney area, causing Fallon's knees to buckle. He tried to reach out for Harn but couldn't as he pitched forward and stretched out in the dirt with no fight left.

Jake staggered to the horse trough and buried his face in the cool water. When he straightened up his shirt was handed to him and on the other end of the shirt were the most beautiful hands of Sarah Garnett.

The barkeep spoke up, "That was some work. Looks to me like you have done some fighting before."

Before Jake could respond, Sarah said, "I don't approve of fighting, but Fallon has been bullying people for some time. He deserved what he got."

"I'm glad that you approved of something that I did," said Jake as he tried to grin through bruised and bloody lips.

Sheriff Ben Mason pushed his way through the crowd and stood next to Jake. He stared at the battered body of Fallon with disbelief on his face. "I never would have believed that."

He turned to Roddy, "Roddy, get Fallon on his horse and get him out of town."

The foreman looked at the sheriff and asked, "What are you going to do about this man almost killing Fallon? He needs a doctor."

"Wash him up in the horse trough and let the housekeeper fix him up. She's done some doctoring," answered the sheriff.

The foreman scowled and said, "I wouldn't want to be in your shoes when Burke finds out that you butted in with his business."

"I'll worry about that when the time comes, and besides, I am trying to keep Harn from killing your man," replied the sheriff. "Now do as you are told."

The foreman helped Fallon stagger to the horse trough and ducked his head in the water. After he came up the foreman handed him a bandana to dry off. He then helped Fallon on his horse and they rode out without another word.

Jake was bleeding from his head, shoulder and battered lips and his knuckles looked like ground meat but he was still trying to smile.

Sarah looked at him and said, "Come on over to the hotel and get yourself cleaned up. I will send for Doc Gray so he can look at you."

"I would love to accept your generous offer but I have an errand to run. "Maybe I'll see you later." He smiled at her weakly and headed off to get his horse.

She stared at Jake for a few moments, shook her head and turned back to the hotel.

Ten

From the information that Jake had been able to gather, two ranchers might be persuaded to join a fight against Burke if the situation was right. Jake had decided to visit the two men, Brad Jason and Trent Cochran. He knew this could be a hard sell but at least he could get an idea about the two men's attitude toward Burke. He headed west out of town, riding past the road leading to the Sterling Ranch. As he rode he remembered the telegram and took it out of his pocket. The envelope was wet with sweat and had some blood splotches, but it was still readable.

He glanced at the words again that said, "Harn: heard Dodge gunman Slade hired kill stranger Burkeville," and it was signed Cranbrook.

He studied the note carefully and shook his head. More trouble coming he told himself. Jake did not understand why Burke would hire Slade to kill him. Obviously, he was the most likely to be killed, but Burke had several gunmen that would be glad to do the job and much cheaper. He put the envelope back in his pocket and rode on.

As he rode he thought about Quincy. He had ignored and tried to get away from the little man, and still he was trying to save Jake's skin. Jake had met many men, some he liked and others he disliked, but Quincy was just different. The little man just had a way of getting under his skin.

A short time later he came up to a stream and pulled Muddy off the road. Muddy needed a drink and Jake certainly needed to wash off some of the dirt and dried blood. He took off his shirt and tried to examine the damage. The bleeding had stopped and Jake knew that the cool water would feel good to his swollen knuckles and face. He washed as well as he could and when he felt that he was presentable, he mounted and rode on.

A half mile or so he came upon a small sign announcing the Jason Ranch. He took the road for a short while and came upon a large meadow with a small stream in the middle. Off to the left was a ranch house, barns, a corral and some small out-buildings. Jake dismounted, took out the makings and built a cigarette as he surveyed the Rocking J spread. He put the cigarette up to his lips and inhaled, it caused some pain and it reminded Jake about the power from the fists of Fallon. His attention went back to the buildings and noticed that they were very well kept, and apparently Brad Jason spent a lot of time making the ranch successful. Jake reasoned that a person that spent this much time on the ranch might very well be willing to defend it.

Jake took a last puff on his cigarette and snuffed it out on the heel of his boot. He mounted, nudged Muddy and they headed on toward the ranch house.

He rode into the yard and noticed that there wasn't anyone outside the house. It was probably too early for the men. Most likely they were still out on the range. He dismounted, walked up the steps on the porch and knocked on the door. A few minutes later a middle-aged woman opened the door. The woman wore a bright colored dress with an apron covering most of it. She was very pretty and in her early years she probably would have been considered beautiful. Jake stared at her for a moment, and she interrupted his thoughts.

Staring at his bruised and swollen face she asked, "How can I help you?"

"Uh, Ma'am, I uh, was looking for Brad Jason," he stammered. Jake was not used to getting caught off guard but he had not expected such an attractive woman at the ranch.

"Mr. uh, who can I tell my husband is calling?" she asked.

Jake recovered his composure and replied, "Jake Harn, Ma'am," and tipped his hat.

"Well, Mr. Harn, come on in, and I will get my husband," she said.

"Thank you, Ma'am," replied Jake. Jake looked around the room and noticed that the inside of the house was as neatly kept as the outside. It surely showed a woman's touch.

A few moments later a tall, slender, middle-aged

man came into the room accompanied by Mrs. Jason. As Jake sized him up he noticed the way that he carried himself. Could have been an army officer, he thought.

Mrs. Jason asked, "Mr. Harn, may I change your bandage before you talk to my husband?"

"Thank you, Ma'am; I'm okay, but thanks for your concern."

"Oh, go ahead and sit down, Harn, she won't take no for an answer," said Mr. Jason.

"Well, okay," replied Jake. He sat down in a chair while Mrs. Jason gathered some white cloth and a wet rag. While she changed his bandages, Mr. Jason introduced himself.

"I'm Brad Jason, and I believe that you have built yourself a reputation in the territory in a very short time," he said.

"Well, Mr. Jason it's not a reputation that I wanted. In fact, I'd planned to stop over-night in Burkeville and move on the next morning," Jake explained.

"I heard about your encounter with Sonny Burke," said Brad, "and I can't say that I'm sorry that he's dead, but I do realize that the killing is causing you some grief. By the looks of your face you have also encountered a grizzly."

"If you are talking about being threatened, getting shot at as well as getting shot, I agree about the grief part," replied Jake. "The grizzly you are talking about was a gent named Fallon."

"Don't tell me that you tangled with Fallon and walked away?" the astonished Jason asked.

"I was lucky," retorted Jake.

Mrs. Jason finished the job and said, "You look much better."

"Thank you, Ma'am," said Jake.

"It had to be more than luck, Harn, Fallon is a killer," replied Jason.

The woman interrupted and said, "Mr. Harn, I have some coffee on the stove if you want to move to the kitchen."

"Mr. Harn, my wife, Mary, will doctor, feed or provide drinks for anyone or anything that shows up at the door of the ranch but, in this case, I think that the drink is a good idea," he replied.

Jason pointed to the wash basin and Jake splashed water on his face and dried off with a nearby towel.

The two men sat down at the kitchen table and Mary Jason poured hot coffee for both. When they were settled, Jason asked Jake, "Harn, what brings you to the Rocking J Ranch?"

"While I was trying to leave town, I was ambushed. Miss Sterling and Sam carried me to the ranch. Since then I've spent the last few days at the Sterling Ranch. I've heard a lot of stories about Jeff Burke and the Bar B Ranch and they are all bad," answered Jake.

Listening to the conversation, Mrs. Jason interrupted, "I don't blame you for spending time at the Sterling Ranch." she laughed and added, "That Rachael is a beautiful, young woman and she works hard helping keep the ranch up."

"Mr. Harn, my wife means well, but she is always trying to find Rachael a husband." explained Brad. "Just ignore her."

"Now, Mr. Harn, you can't tell me that you haven't looked at her," Mary said.

Jake was seldom embarrassed but now his face turned red and he said, "Yes ma'am, she is a beautiful woman." He was certainly not going to tell Mrs. Jason about all of the thoughts that he had concerning Rachael.

"Harn, just ignore her and go on with your story," said Jason.

"Yes, well I have spoken to the Sterlings and the sheriff, and I am trying to get enough men to work out a plan that I have in mind that may help the smaller ranchers."

"Since no one has enough men, it may be difficult to do."

"Mr. Jason, I am not planning to face off with Burke and his gunmen, I want to get his men distracted and capture Jeff Burke and take him to Hays City for trial," said Jake.

"Why Hayes City?" questioned Jason.

"Hays City is close to Fort Hayes. The city was built by Union Pacific Railroad dollars and the law is more likely to cooperate. The business climate would suffer without strict enforcement of the laws."

"Even if you can get him to Hays City, what makes you think that the authorities will press charges against him?" asked Jason. "Burke is a rich and powerful man."

"I got some information from Sheriff Ben Mason about the story at Jones Crossing where Sonny Burke killed a man, but the old man got him off," explained Jake.

"What information?" asked Jason.

I don't know exactly, but I plan to go to Jones Crossing and talk to the sheriff and, if what I think is true, it may be much easier to get him held for trial.

"I still don't follow you," said Jason.

"I was a deputy for a short period and I got to know the district judge. I believe that I can get Burke held, at least for trial, and we can put together a case as we go. Hopefully, if Burke is in jail, some of his victims will come forward and testify against him," explained Jake.

"Harn, you are taking a big risk that might get you killed," replied Jason.

"I admit there is a risk, but I don't have a better plan."

"Let's say that I throw in with you, what would you want me to do, considering the fact that I only have four men on the payroll?" asked Jason.

"How well do you know Trent Cochran and the other ranchers?" asked Jake.

Jason answered, "I know Cochran very well but the others are only causal acquaintances."

"I would like for you to get in touch with the other ranchers and explain the plan and find out if they will stand with us. I got the impression that you have military experience, is that correct?" asked Jake.

"Correct, Captain of the 1st Ohio Cavalry serving under Colonel Owen P. Ransom," replied Jason. "I fought at Chickamauga, Missionary Ridge and other campaigns."

"I was on the other side and spent many hellish days including places such as Cold Harbor and Antietam—places that before the war I didn't know they even existed."

"Many good men fought and died in places that were not even on the map before the war," acknowledged Jason, "and many had no idea why they were fighting."

"Well, we won't win any debates over the right and wrongs of that issue, but here is the plan and if you can get enough men, you could head up a group and keep them from getting themselves killed," answered Jake.

"There are many good men from both sides of that conflict living around here and we all usually get along very well. I will see what I can do. How can I get in touch with you?" asked Jason.

"It might be risky to contact me personally so get word to the sheriff if it's a go." replied Jake. "Good luck and be very careful."

"I will do whatever I can to protect my ranch."

"Okay, this is what I want you to do," said Jake. He explained the plan that he had in mind and told Jason that he had already asked for help from the sheriff. Jason agreed to pay a visit to the other ranchers and report back to the sheriff. When all of the details about the plan were discussed, Jake rose to go.

"Thanks for your help and I'll be in touch," said Jake.

"I just hope your plan works. If not, we may be moving out soon," replied Jason.

Jake nodded to Jason and said, "Thanks for the coffee, Mrs. Jason."

"You're welcome. And keep in mind about what I said about Miss Sterling," she replied.

"Mary, leave him alone, the man has more important things to think about," replied Jason.

Jake smiled and nodded to Mary Jason and said, "I'll keep your advice in mind."

The rancher escorted Jake out of the house and said that he would do whatever he could to make the plan work. Jake nodded, mounted Muddy and headed for Jones Crossing.

Eleven

Jake pondered. If his hunch was correct he might be able to get information that he could take to the federal marshals that couldn't be ignored. If his hunch was incorrect he could be up the creek without a paddle. A few hours ride to Jones Crossing could decide things one way or the other.

Jones Crossing was little more than a half-day's ride, and Jake figured that he could be there just before dark. Muddy was rested and anxious to be on the trail again so Jake rode on at a gallop. After hard riding for a couple of hours, Jake reined in at a small water hole with some surrounding shade trees. He loosed the cinch on the saddle, took the Henry out of the scabbard, and led Muddy to the water hole. After he drank his fill, Jake took his turn. He moved Muddy to a grassy spot where he could graze and dropped the reins. Jake pulled out some beef jerky and ate enough to hold back the hunger pangs until he reached Jones Crossing.

He built a smoke and thought about how he was going to get the information that he needed. Sheriff Mason had said that the Jones Crossing sheriff was a reasonable man, so he decided to approach him first. His first thought was to confront the judge directly, but he quickly abandoned that idea in favor of the visit with Sheriff Tom Benson. Benson was the arresting officer and should know everything about the incident.

Jake took a last puff on the smoke and winched when the cigarette touched his tender lip. He exhaled the smoke and ground the butt under his heel. He slipped the Henry back into the scabbard, climbed aboard Muddy and rode on. Jones Crossing was some larger than Burkeville. It had two saloons and two restaurants along with a hotel, a General Store and a bathhouse and some other buildings that he couldn't quickly recognize.

The aches and pains from the fight with Fallon cried out for a hot bath and bed, but Jake's first chore was to have a word with the sheriff. He just hoped that the sheriff would be willing to share all of the information he had about the killing of Sonny Burke and maybe even why he was not prosecuted.

The sheriff's office was between the barber shop and the general store. Jake had just reined in at the hitching rail in front of the office, when out came an older man with a badge pinned to his chest.

Jake looked at the man and said, "Sheriff Tom Benson, I assume."

"That's me, but you got me because I don't know who you are," replied the sheriff.

"My name is Jake Harn, I just rode in from Burkeville. I would like a word with you."

"Well, Jake Harn, my first question is what wild animal did you tangle with and before you answer, my second question is: I was just stepping out for supper, would you like to join me?" asked the sheriff.

"Sheriff, you can call me Jake."

"Okay, Jake, now how about some supper?"

Jake's stomach had been gnawing for some time, and he was happy to accept the sheriff's invitation. The long ride coupled with the fight against Fallon had worn him out.

"The wild animal's name was Fallon. He didn't like my appearance and wanted to run me out of town as a favor to Jeff Burke."

The sheriff looked at Jake more closely and said, "Come on, maybe some food and hot coffee will help. Obviously you are not the first person that tangled with Fallon but you appear to have come out better than most."

"You know Fallon?"

"Saw him a few times but I steered as far from him as I could."

The two walked down the street to the Crossing Café and walked in. The crowd was beginning to arrive, but the waitress guided the two to a corner table. When they sat down the sheriff nodded to the waitress and said, "Thanks, Rosy."

"And who is this handsome stranger?" asked Rosy.

"This gent calls himself Jake Harn, bruises and all,"

said Sheriff Benson, "but I have no idea who he is or what he is doing in Jones Crossing."

"Well, when you are finished with him send him to me and I'll care for him bruises and all," said Rosy with a chuckle.

"Behave yourself and bring us some coffee along with some grub," said the sheriff with a grin.

She smiled at Jake and hurried to the kitchen.

"Now, Mr. Harn, what can I do for you?"

"Interested in a shooting that took place some time ago and involved Sonny Burke."

"I'm very familiar with it, what's your interest in the shooting?" asked the sheriff. "And before you answer, I know that you killed Sonny."

"I can't deny that. Unfortunately, when I rode into Burkeville, Sonny Burke called me out, and I had to kill him. Now Jeff Burke is trying to kill me. That's not all. He is trying to drive out all of the smaller ranchers from the territory. He wants to own all of the land for himself."

"The long arm of the Burke Ranch reaches far and wide, including Jones Crossing," replied the sheriff.

"My understanding is that Sonny Burke killed an unarmed man in your town and he got off scot free."

"That's basically true," explained the sheriff. "Sonny goaded a cowboy named Shorty Hall. When Shorty got really mad, Sonny slid him a gun down the bar but Shorty would not reach for the gun. Burke shot him anyway. I knew Shorty for many years, and he never even carried a gun. Doubt that he ever owned one."

"What provoked the shooting?"

"Apparently Shorty had a regular relationship with one of the saloon girls and Sonny was horning in. Shorty was mad and made some comments to Burke, but he knew that he could not fight Sonny Burke and win," replied the sheriff.

"I'm assuming that there were witnesses. What happened after the shooting?" asked Jake.

"Yes, there were witnesses, so my deputy and I arrested Sonny and put him in jail. Two days later the judge ordered him released."

"Why?" asked Jake.

"The judge claimed that there was not enough evidence to hold him, so he ordered him released before an inquest could be held."

The coffee came along with steak, potatoes and bread. The two men settled down and began devouring the meal. Rosy smiled at Jake and said, "Okay, Handsome, if you need anything else just call me."

"I'll do it," replied Jake.

"How 'bout me?" asked the sheriff.

"You had your chances," she winked at the sheriff and headed toward the kitchen.

Jake caught the nod and winks between Rosy and the sheriff and decided that there was more than a casual relationship between the two. He decided he didn't blame the sheriff, that Rosy was a handsome woman.

They ate in silence until they cleared their plates and Rosy brought refills for the coffee.

"Much obliged, Ma'am, I was sure starving," said Jake as she finished filling his cup.

She smiled and walked away exaggerating her hips. The sheriff's eyes followed her every step until she disappeared into the kitchen.

Jake interrupted the silence and asked the sheriff, "Anything else you can tell me about the shooting?"

"The only thing that I know is that Old Man Burke visited the judge before the decision was made."

"Were you there when the meeting took place?"

"No, and the judge would not answer any questions about the meeting," answered the sheriff.

"Thanks, Sheriff, perhaps you could steer me to the local hotel. I don't feel like camping out, and I would like to meet the judge. Would the judge be in town tomorrow?"

"Well, there is only one hotel in town and it is just down the block. The judge is in town now and will be for a few more days. He spends a week or so a month in Jones Crossing," replied the sheriff.

"Much obliged sheriff. By the way, where would I be able to get a hot bath?" asked Jake.

"Just beyond the hotel, just ask for Pepe," replied the sheriff.

Jake nodded, left some coins on the table and strolled out of the café. He stopped outside the door and rolled a smoke. He inhaled deeply and watched the activity on the street. He looked at the general store and decided that it was time for some new clothing. He put out the cigarette and headed to the store. He selected a new shirt and trousers, paid the clerk, and headed to the hotel.

He walked in and spoke to the desk clerk who handed Jake the key to a room and he turned to go, "By the way, where can I find Pepe?"

"Out the side door to the next building, knock on the door. He likes to sleep a lot so he may be napping, knock hard," replied the clerk.

Jake took his saddle bags and rifle to the room and laid them on the bed. After looking around, he headed for the bath house. Pepe appeared when Jake knocked and he readied the hot water. Jake took off the bandage on his head that Mrs. Jason had put on and decided that he could do without it.

He paid for the bath and spent an hour or so just soaking. It felt good to get the trail dust off his body, and it helped soothe his recent aches and pains. He dressed in the new clothes, wrapped up the old ones, and walked over to the livery stable to check on Muddy. Muddy nipped at Jake and Jake slapped him lightly on his forehead. "You ornery cayuse. I guess we didn't ride far enough today to suit you." He stuffed the old clothes in his saddle bag and looked back at the horse.

Muddy whinnied and nodded his head as Jake turned to leave. Jake decided that a beer was in order, and he walked down the street to the Crossing Saloon. The room was quite full, Jake walked up to the bar and shouldered between two cowboys that apparently had been drinking for some time. The gent on the left stared at Jake, but the other apparently didn't know that he was jostled.

The bartender sidled up to Jake. He was short and stout with a large mustache that covered most of his mouth. He looked Jake up and down and asked, "What'll you have Mister?

"Beer."

The bartender came back with the beer and Jake gave him a five piece. Jake drank it down and ordered another. Just as he was lifting the second mug, someone bumped his arm and caused Jake to spill part of the contents onto the bar.

Jake turned around and came face to face with a short young man with fancy clothing and two guns on his gun belt. They were tied down in the fashion of a professional gunman.

He glared at Jake. "Why don't you watch what you're doing?"

Jake stared at him for a moment and said, "Kid, where I come from it's customary to apologize when you bump into someone."

"Ole man, I don't apologize to nobody for nothin'," shouted the kid. The kid was a little unsteady on his feet and his speech was slurred.

"Alcohol sometimes does strange things to a person, Kid. My suggestion is that you go somewhere and sleep off the alcohol before you get killed," replied Jake.

"You suggesting that I'm drunk?"

"I just call 'em the way I see 'em," replied Jake.

"I've killed men for saying less," said the kid.

"Kid, I have no quarrel with you so let's just drop it."

"You're scared."

"Boy, I've met a lot of young punks just like you. You're a loud mouth, and you pick on saddle tramps and people that can't defend themselves and you scratch a notch on your gun when you kill 'em. Well, you're picking on someone that doesn't give a damn about your reputation."

The kid's face turned beet red, and he reached for his gun and said, "Why you son–of–a–b…"

Anticipating the move, Jake backhanded the kid in the mouth. The force from his right hand knocked him sprawling in the corner on the floor. The kid looked up at Jake with his gun half out of his holster.

"Friend, if you've a hankering to die, go right ahead and draw," said Jake.

Just as the kid was pulling leather, a big boot stepped on his hand.

"Leave it be, Tagg. It's not worth dying for," said Sheriff Tom Benson.

"Nobody hits me and gets away with it," shouted the angry young man.

Jake kept his eye on the kid on the floor, but the sheriff disarmed him and had a couple of bystanders escort him to the jail. The sheriff spoke to Jake, "I can keep him locked up until tomorrow afternoon but you need to be careful. He considers himself a gunny. He's quite good with a gun and he's crazy enough to draw on anyone."

"How about when he's sober?" asked Jake.

"Unfortunately, he's seldom sober."

"Much obliged, Sheriff. I will try and be gone before you let him out," replied Jake.

Jake finished his beer and turned to leave. "Good luck with the judge," said the sheriff.

Jake waved his hand, walked out of the saloon, headed to the hotel, and climbed the stairs to his room.

Twelve

Roddy now knew what he imagined Dave Egan and Ike felt when they had to face Burke after their encounter with Jake Harn. Roddy had worked for the Burke ranch for many years but he knew that in spite of all that time he was going to get a tongue lashing by Jeff Burke. Burke was impatient, and he hated failure from any of his men. Roddy had thought many times that he would just ride out and go on west to Colorado or even down to Texas.

But he realized that even thinking about it was absurd because Burke would not let him leave. Besides, with all of his faults, Burke paid much more money than he could make anywhere else.

Fallon was moaning and flopping on his horse, and Roddy decided that he might fall off and knew he would never be able to get him back up. He stopped the horses and dismounted. He spoke to Fallon, who now appeared to be somewhat coherent.

"Want to get down?" asked the foreman.

"Hell yes, I want off of this thing. You know I hate horses."

The foreman didn't say anything but just slipped the knot from the rope and helped the big man down.

His legs were wobbly but he stayed on his feet. "Where the hell are we, and why are we out of town?"

"Harn beat the hell out of you and the damn sheriff told me to get you out of town," replied Roddy.

"I am going to kill that bastard Harn and that stupid sheriff too."

"Take it easy big man. You're not going to do much fighting anytime soon."

Fallon sat down on a grassy spot and then stretched out flat on his back. "What are we going to do now?"

"There is a small stream a little ways off. I am going to try and clean you up before we have to face the boss."

Fallon moaned and said, "I don't want to see him."

"Well, I have to and so do you. Just lay here while I get some water."

The foreman walked to the water hole and dipped his hat in the water. He brought it back to where Fallon was laying and sat it down. He took his bandana, dipped it into the water and proceeded to clean up the big man as well as he could.

After he had finished he got him back on the horse and rode on toward the ranch. Fallon groaned and moaned like he was going to die, but the foreman ignored him. His mind was occupied thinking about what he was going to say to Burke.

The trip was too short to suit him, and they soon reached the ranch. They rode up to the bunk house and the foreman dismounted.

"Kid," he motioned to the gent that called himself the Apache Kid. "Give me some help getting Fallon off."

The kid looked at Fallon and at the foreman. "What happened to him?"

"Harn beat the hell out of him," replied the foreman. "Now help me get him down."

The two got the big man off the horse and led him to the horse trough. Fallon took the hint and ducked his head into the trough. He dried his face and looked at the foreman. "Let's go see the boss."

The two men walked up the steps to the ranch house and went in. The foreman hesitated at Burke's office door and then knocked.

"Come in," hollered Burke.

The foreman opened the door, stepped in and stood aside while Fallon walked in. Burke was working on papers on his desk and smoking a cigar. He looked up from his work and dropped his cigar when he saw the battered and bruised face of the big man. He looked at Roddy and asked, "What the hell happened to him?"

The foreman explained what had happened in the saloon and on the street and just as he was finishing Fallon interrupted, "I'm gonna kill that bastard Harn."

Burke looked at Fallon disgustedly and replied, "You had your chance and Harn beat the hell out of you. Can't I get anyone that can do what I want done?"

"Boss, I…"

Burke interrupted the big man and looked at the foreman, "Get him something to eat and take him to the bunkhouse. Maybe Jack Slade can finish the job."

Thirteen

Jake woke up early, dressed and walked to the livery stable to check on Muddy. The horse had already been fed and watered, so he was happy to see Jake. Jake spent some time with him and then headed for the café. It was too early for a large crowd but Rosy was there and preparing for the day's business. He found a seat in the back corner and waited for her.

"Morning, Handsome, up awful early this morn'," she greeted Jake with a smile.

Are you flirting with me?" he asked with a mischievous grin.

"I sure am, I flirt with all of the handsome men that come in," she replied. "By the way, you look a sight better than yesterday."

"Thank you, Rosy, I feel a lot better. You mean until the sheriff ties you down?"

"What do you mean?" she said.

"You'll flirt with all the men until the sheriff corrals you."

Rosy turned serious for a moment and replied, "That tying down part may take a long time. Oh well, that's my problem. What can I get you for breakfast?"

"Steak and eggs with coffee," said Jake.

Her smile reappeared and she said, "Comin' right up."

A few minutes later the food appeared and Rosy joked with Jake while she poured the coffee. Jake thanked her and spent several minutes eating and leisurely drinking coffee. He paid for breakfast and left the café.

His first priority was to see the judge, but Jake knew that he wouldn't be in the office this early. Instead he decided to head for the general store. He purchased supplies, including the makings, told the clerk that he would pick them up later and left the store. On the porch he built a smoke and gazed down the street. Not many people were in sight. He finished the cigarette and headed for the sheriff's office. Jake stepped inside expecting to see the sheriff but instead was greeted by another man wearing a badge.

"Mornin'," said the man, "What can I do for you?"

"Lookin' for the sheriff," replied Harn.

"Not come in yet, I'm Deputy Pete Durkok."

"Glad to meet you Pete. Name is Jake Harn; I'm interested in finding the judge."

"You probably won't find him this early, but his office is two doors past the bank. Keeps an office there when he's in town," replied the deputy.

"What time does he normally get to his office?"

"Its seven thirty so he'll probably be in 'bout eight. Coffee's on, want some?"

"Love some."

The deputy poured coffee for Jake and himself and they talked for some minutes while they drank. After Jake finished his coffee he handed the cup to the deputy. "Thanks for the coffee."

"Not at all."

Jake started for the door then hesitated and turned back to the deputy. "By the way, were you with the sheriff when Sonny Burke killed Shorty?"

"Sure was, I've been with the sheriff for nigh on three years," he replied.

"Much obliged, Pete, I may want to talk to you a little later if you don't mind."

"Be glad to help," replied Pete.

Jake nodded and walked out onto the street. He turned left out of the sheriff's office and headed toward the judge's office just a few steps past the bank. The sign read Judge Ben Robichaux. Jake knocked on the door, walked in without waiting for a response, and looked at the judge sitting behind a wooden desk. On the desk top were papers strewn all over.

The judge looked up but did not speak. Jake waited until he put down the paper and pen and said, "I'm Jake Harn. Need to have a word with you if you are Judge Ben Robichaux."

"I am," he replied, "but, as you can see, I'm very busy."

"I'll try to be brief, Judge," said Jake.

The judge pointed to one of the chairs along the wall and said, "Take a seat."

Jake nodded, pulled a chair closer to the desk and dropped into it.

"Now, what can I do for you?" asked the judge.

Jake briefly explained the events that had taken place since he rode into the town of Burkeville. He stressed the shooting of Sonny Burke and Old Man Burke's vow to kill Jake, and then he spoke to the judge. "I am not as concerned about these matters as I am the Burkes' gunmen trying to run out all the smaller ranchers," he said.

"And what do you want from me?"

"Well, let me explain..."

The judge interrupted Jake and asked, "And what is your connection to the ranchers?"

"I believe that when someone tries to steal other people's property it should be your business and mine. Besides, members of the Sterling Ranch were very kind to me, and I'd hate for anything to happen to them," answered Jake.

"So why are you telling me this?" asked the judge.

"For some time now Jeff Burke has been involved in looting, killing and trying to force people out of the territory so he can take over their land. On top of that, I believe that Burke bribed a judge to get his son off on a murder charge and that's where you come in," replied Jake.

"Harn, I don't like your accusations, and I'll not listen to anymore," he said, raising his voice.

"Judge, I assure you that I'm not concerned about you or your past, my only goal is to protect the small ranches and take down Jeff Burke if necessary," replied Jake.

"What do you know about my past?"

"There are rumors that you had some problems in New Orleans and that you left under the cover of darkness. I suspect that a telegram to the authorities would allow anyone to get the details."

"Harn, this is blackmail, and I can have you put in jail."

"Judge, I've already stated my concern. Burke is ruthless and will do almost anything to get what he wants. I spoke to the sheriff, and he told me that the evidence against Sonny Burke was a cinch to get him hanged, yet you let him go. That means that Burke bought you off or blackmailed you to get his son off. If you want to file charges against me, go right ahead."

"Get out of my office, Harn."

"Judge, I have no intention of leaving until I get the answers I need."

"I will call the sheriff and have you removed."

"Judge, I've spoken to the sheriff, and I think that he also is waiting for some answers."

The judge stared at Jake and decided that he was not going to get rid of this brash cowboy. He leaned over his desk with his head in his hands and said, "I didn't want to let him go, but I had to."

"Sonny?" asked Jake.

"Yes, Old Man Burke found out that I shot a man in New Orleans, and he threatened to notify the authorities."

"Why would Burke be able to blackmail you?"

"Because I never told anyone."

"And so you just left town."

"I didn't have a choice."

"The man that you shot, did he die?" asked Jake.

"I don't know. I left before the word got out. I was an attorney in the city, with a promising future, until I got mixed up with the wrong woman." Tears came to his eyes as he related the story.

"You don't have to tell me everything, I just want you to write a letter about the incident with Burke and the bribery," said Jake.

"That will ruin my career."

"Judge, your career may very well be over anyway."

"If this gets out, I may go to jail in addition to ruining my career."

"That could be, but it has to be done," replied Jake.

The Judge was silent for a few moments and then he said, "This has been on my mind for a long time and I've not told anyone. Maybe it is time." He took a few moments to gather his thoughts and began. "I struck up a friendship with a prominent New Orleans banker. His wife was several years younger than her husband and she flirted with me incessantly. One night I gave in and while he was away we made love. Unfortunately, he came home early and caught us in the bedroom. He went berserk, I panicked and shot him. The very same night I packed a few things and left town." Jake listened as the judge went on. "After some time drifting I landed here, started a law practice and later was appointed a district judge. Harn, I know that it doesn't matter, but that is the only time that I misused my position."

"Judge, people make mistakes, but there has to be consequences, even for judges," replied Jake.

"Harn, I appreciate you listening. If you'll send the sheriff to my office I'll write the letter that you want and you can get it from him."

"Thanks, Judge, goodbye and good luck." Jake walked out of the office. He stopped outside the door, took out the makings and rolled a cigarette. He was trying to decide whether he wanted coffee first or the talk with the sheriff. The decision was made easy when the sheriff walked out of the telegraph office and headed toward Jake. Jake drew deeply on the cigarette, inhaled and blew out the smoke then crushed the cigarette under his heel.

As the sheriff walked near he asked, "Any luck with the judge?"

"Yes, and he wants to speak with you in his office," Jake replied.

"Now what did you do, get me in trouble?" he quipped.

Jake grinned at the sheriff and said "Meet me at the café after you talk with him and I'll buy you coffee."

As Jake walked into the café he looked for Rosy, but she was not around. An older lady brought the coffee and Jake drank it while waiting for the sheriff. A good bit later the sheriff walked in with an envelope in his hand. He sat down at the table and handed the letter to Jake. Jake took the envelope without speaking, then read the letter and tucked it inside his shirt.

"By the way, Harn, you might want to know that the judge is leaving Jones Crossing and going back to New Orleans," said the sheriff. The waitress brought coffee for the sheriff and then warmed up Jake's cup.

"I sorta feel sorry for the judge," said Jake.

"Well, I wouldn't feel too sorry for him," the sheriff said as he produced a telegram from his shirt pocket."

"What do you mean?" asked Jake.

"I contacted the New Orleans police after we spoke yesterday evening and I just got the answer back. The banker that the judge shot was not seriously injured and under questioning he admitted that he pulled a gun on the judge first. It is doubtful that he will serve much jail time."

"Did you tell the judge?" asked Jake.

"No, he grinned sheepishly, I thought that I would tell him after he gets on the stage."

Jake nodded in understanding and said, "Sheriff, I've some riding to do. Thanks for your help and keep that kid locked up until I get out of town."

"Will do and good luck." said the sheriff. "And stop and see me if you are in town again."

"Much obliged."

Jake paid for the coffee and headed for the general store. After picking up his supplies he walked down the street to the livery stable. He knew that Muddy was waiting impatiently to get on the trail. Jake was also anxious because the ride was several hours long and he wanted to get there before dark.

Fourteen

Jack Slade had a long ride from Dodge City to Burkeville and, as was always his custom, his first stop was the nearest saloon. He tied his horse at the rail in front of the Trail's End Saloon, rolled a cigarette, and looked around. In the case of Burkeville, there were no options because the town only had one drinking establishment. It was just before dusk and Slade knew that he had plenty of drinking time before bedding down for the night.

Slade had received a telegram from Jeff Burke offering him a job. He was busy but the price that Burke quoted was above that for the normal job. Slade only worked in one field, and the one that Burke offered was his specialty. Burke wanted a man killed. Slade had killed several men, most of them for pay. The message that he received did not give his victim's name, but the story had spread about Jake Harn killing Burke's son. Slade assumed that this was the reason for the telegram and, if so, he was familiar with Harn. The two had met in the Long Branch Saloon in Dodge City some weeks back. Slade had no quarrel with Harn, but he didn't need a quarrel when the money was good. In this case, $500 was a lot of money, and Slade needed a lot of money to maintain his current life style. He wore fancy clothes, rode an expensive horse and carried two Walker Colts that would cost the average cowhand two months wages. He also had expensive tastes in alcohol and women.

Slade took a last drag on his cigarette, put it out and walked into the saloon. He looked around and stepped up to the bar. With a loud voice he hollered, "Barkeep, a bottle of your best whiskey." The bartender was busy with other customers, but quickly turned at the voice. Pat, the bartender, had been in the business for a long time and he had been in many different towns over the years. He had met a lot of people but this voice he recognized immediately. It was Jack Slade. "Right away, Mr. Slade," he replied.

"Hurry up, I don't have all night," retorted Slade.

The bartender remembered that Slade was always in a hurry and that he did not take pity on anyone that did not do his bidding. Pat brought a full bottle and a clean glass and set them on the bar in front of Slade. Slade examined the bottle and said, "I only drink the best."

"Mr. Slade, this is the best, and you should know that I only serve the best," replied Pat.

"How do you know my name?" asked Slade.

"I tended bar in a saloon in Juniper Springs a few years ago when you came in," replied Pat.

Slade looked at Pat and examined the bottle again

and poured a double into the glass. He tipped the glass and swallowed the whisky with one gulp. He nodded to Pat and poured another drink. The bartender walked away to tend to other customers.

Slade swallowed the second drink, picked up the bottle and glass and headed for the corner table that was occupied by three cowboys. He stopped and stood behind one of the cowboys. "I'm taking this table, and I'd suggest that you three move elsewhere."

The cowboy turned and asked, "Who you talking to, Mister?"

"I'm talking to you, Friend, and I don't waste words when I want something," snarled Slade.

The cowboy looked at Slade again and said, "I'd suggest that you find your own table."

Slade touched his guns, backed up a couple steps and said, "Mister, you move or your friends will carry your body out to Boot Hill."

The cowboy stood up and faced Slade. "Maybe you'll be the one being carried out," he replied.

The bartender hollered at Rusty, "Move to another table and let him have that table before you get killed."

Slade ignored the bartender and said to the man called Rusty, "If you're calling my play, you have a gun. Reach for it when you're ready to die."

Just at that moment, Jake Harn walked into the saloon. He heard the comment from Slade and recognized the voice. Jake had no idea how good the man called

Rusty was with a gun but he had seen Slade in action. He thought for a moment and decided that something good could come out of this if he could keep Slade from killing Rusty and or his friends. He would have to act quickly and he did. He moved closer, looked at Rusty and said, "Friend, I'd like to buy you a drink for the help you gave me a few days ago."

Slade looked at Jake and said, "Harn, I thought that you skipped town."

"Sorry to disappoint you, Slade."

"Harn this is not your fight, just stand down."

"Slade, I'm not looking for a fight, I'm just inviting my friend to have a drink," retorted Jake. "And if you kill him I'd be disappointed."

The bartender stepped behind the cowboy and said to him, "Rusty, there is no reason for you to get killed, and I know that you don't want to face Jack Slade."

Rusty turned pale at the mention of Jack Slade, but tried to keep his composure. "No one can tell me where I can sit," he said.

"Keep out of this, Barkeep, the man wants to die and I'm going to accommodate him."

Jake Harn moved closer to the table and to the other side of Rusty and he said, "You and your two friends can have a drink at the bar on me."

The bartender quickly added, "Come on boys, come up to the bar and you all can have a drink on the house."

Rusty looked at Slade, grudgingly but started walking toward the bar. Rusty knew that he was not the fastest gun around, but he had his pride and he heard Slade snickering in the background. He started to turn toward Slade but Jake nudged him on toward the bar. Slade put his glass and bottle on the table and sat down as the other two cowboys joined Jake and Rusty at the bar. The bartender walked back behind the bar and asked, "What'll you have, Gents?"

"Whiskey," said Rusty and the other cowboys nodded in agreement.

"Beer for me," said Jake.

"I have some very fine whiskey if you would prefer to change your mind," said the bartender.

"No thanks, Barkeep, I don't drink anything stronger." The bartender brought the drinks and stayed close to where they were standing.

The four men sipped their drinks, and after awhile Rusty looked at Jake, "How did you know that this guy was Jack Slade?"

"I met Slade in Dodge City a few weeks ago. He was looking for a man in Dodge. He caught up to him and killed him. Soon after that I left town," replied Jake.

"Anyway, thanks for saving my hide, I have a temper and sometimes it gets me in trouble," he said.

Jake looked at the three cowboys and said, "I've just finished a long ride, and I am starved. You boys can repay me by having dinner with me at the café and listening to a proposition."

Rusty looked at the other two and answered Jake, "I guess that we owe you that much, but as you probably know we are short on funds."

"Dinner is on me."

"Well, that settles it, come on, Boys."

Jake nodded toward the bartender and turned toward the door.

"Gents, if you think this is the end of it, you're crazy," said Slade.

Jake looked at the three cowboys to be sure they wouldn't respond. He glanced back at Slade, then they walked out of the saloon.

Fifteen

J ake and the three men walked across the street to the café and took a corner table. Shortly, Johnny came in from the kitchen and approached the four men. "What'll you have?" she asked.

Rusty said, "When I've been in before you only had stew, do we have anything other than stew?"

"Well, we did but since you are so late, you will have to eat stew again," she replied.

Rusty looked at her and kidded Johnny, "I think that the only thing you ever serve is stew."

"Rusty, I've seen you around town for awhile now, and I'm not sure that you could even afford to buy the stew," she answered, "but for your information we usually have steak and potatoes."

"Okay, Johnny, let's have steak and potatoes for everybody and see if you can rustle up some bread and coffee too," Jake said.

"I hope that one of you good-for-nothings has money to pay for the food," Johnny said and winked at Jake. Before anyone could answer, she waddled off to the kitchen.

After several minutes of small talk, Jake explained what happened to him and the trouble that he had with the three men from Burkes Ranch. He then told them about the mixed brands in the valley.

Rusty declared, "Everyone in the area knows that Burke controls most of the land now and plans to control everything in the future. That means that Burke and his men control everything that happens in these parts, so there is no doubt that they are responsible for rustling the cattle."

Steve, one of the cowboys, added, "Anyone around here would be a fool to cut in on Burke's plans."

The other man added, "The cattle most likely will be hidden for a while and then driven over to Cottonwood Falls. Burke has plenty of men to drive the cattle. There's very little law there and the cattle can be held for days or sold off fast."

"I'm sure that you are both right but apparently there's no one in the county that can stop Burke," answered Jake, "unless the ranchers can hire some additional men. By the way, I can't help but notice that you guys have not hired on with Burke or any of the other ranchers."

"At one point we worked for the Burke ranch but it was much different then. We moved on to the Hawkins Ranch but he sold out under pressure from Burke. We thought about leaving town but just never got around to it," replied Rusty.

"Well, this may be your chance to get a job here," said Jake.

"Where?"

"The Sterling Ranch."

"Are you sayin' that you're going to get even more involved in a fight against Burke?" asked Rusty.

"Rusty, I'm already involved, I killed two men including Sonny Burke, and I was shot, most likely by someone from the Burke Ranch," Jake answered. "And Burke has vowed to kill me and most likely hired Slade to make sure that it happens."

"Wouldn't it be the smart thing for you to do to get out of the county as quick as you can?" asked Rusty. "Steve here is an excellent guide and tracker and he knows every inch of this territory."

"I'd be glad to get you out and we could even go with you," replied Steve.

"I appreciate your help and advice, but the Sterling Ranch has been good to me over the past few days. They could have left me on the trail to die. Instead they cared for me even when they knew that Burke was looking for me. Besides, I'm not the kind of person that sneaks out of town," replied Jake.

"Harn, does this stubbornness have anything to do with Jim Sterling's daughter? She sure is a looker!" Rusty said with a smile.

"Rusty, I agree with your assessment about Miss Sterling but there is more to it than her."

"Rusty, leave the man alone. He is not going to tell you anything anyway," said Billy. Then, turning to Jake, continued, "Well, if we decided to hire on, we're not really gun hands. How could we help?"

"Billy, I'm not really looking for gun hands. What the Sterling's need right now are some additional cow hands for the ranch," he explained.

Before any more conversation, Johnny brought hot steaming plates of steak, potatoes, bread and coffee. The conversation died as the four men concentrated on the meal. Jake watched his three companions and decided that this must have been the best meal that they had had for some time. After the food was eaten, they sat at the table drinking coffee.

Jake interrupted the silence by addressing the three, "I spoke to Sheriff Ben Mason and he suggested that you three were pretty good cowhands and also pretty good with a gun."

"Look, Jake, I appreciate what you did for me, but Burke has probably thirty gunmen on his payroll. Billy, Steve, and I are pretty good hands with cattle and we do alright with guns," he continued, "but bucking Jeff Burke in a range war is another issue all together," said Rusty.

"I understand how you feel, but you've made an enemy already and, as I said before, I think that Burke hired Slade," replied Jake. "If my hunch is right, you may have made an enemy of Jeff Burke also."

Rusty scratched his chin and answered "I guess what you say is true."

Billy chimed in, "Jake, are you saying that Rusty is in trouble with the Burkes because of the run-in with Slade?"

"Billy, I know Jack Slade, and he's a killer. He gets paid for being a killer, but he also enjoys killing people that get in his way, and Rusty got in his way. It is my guess that he is in danger regardless of Jeff Burke," explained Jake. "As for your suggestion about running, you and I might be able to get out of the county but how about the other ranchers? I spoke with Brad Jason and he is going to meet with the other ranchers. He may be able to persuade them to throw in together and make a stand against Burke," said Jake.

"Harn, if you are expecting help from those ranchers you may be disappointed," replied Steve.

"Are you boys acquainted with any of the other ranchers?" asked Jake.

"I know most of the riders and that's why you may not get any help. None of them will be much good when the Bar B gunmen start throwing lead," replied Steve.

"That's a risk that we have to take if we are going to stay in the territory," answered Jake.

Rusty said, "Well, Boys, I think that I will tag along with Mr. Harn if there is any bunkhouse space at the Sterling Ranch."

"I was hoping that you'd say that. You can pick your bunk. I am sure that Jim Sterling will be glad to put you up for a while," replied Jake. He looked at Steve and Billy and said, "There is a risk, so if you choose not to do it, no hard feelings."

"We've been together for a long time." Steve looked at Billy, the younger man, and asked, "How about it?"

Both men agreed to try it for a while, and Jake suggested that they go to the hotel, get their gear and meet at the stable.

Jake paid the bill and just as the four men reached the door it opened, and in walked Jack Slade. He noticed Rusty and the others and he said to Rusty, "Remember, we still have some unfinished business to take care of."

Jake stared at Slade and coldly remarked, "Slade, since these men are working with me now, all business that you might have to discuss will have to go through me. If you are talking about gun play, that too will have to go through me."

"Harn, if I decide to come for you I want you to sweat first," he said.

"Slade, you are only waiting to get paid by Burke before you try to do your killing. I wonder what the going-price for a killing is these days?" added Jake.

Slade skirted the question, "I don't know anyone named Burke and I do my own business whether or not I get paid," he snarled and walked toward a table in the corner of the café.

When they were outside on the sidewalk, Rusty

scolded Jake, "Why do you want to rile him when you know that he's a killer?"

Jake pondered the question and replied, "Rusty, sometimes people that are riled will become angry and frustrated and then they make mistakes that can get them killed."

"He doesn't seem to be the type that rattles easy," said Rusty. "Just be careful."

The three cowboys headed toward the hotel and Jake went in the other direction toward the livery stable. He found Old Jed the livery man, paid for Muddy's keep then took him out of his stall. The horse was always happy to see Jake but he didn't want Jake to know it. Jake saddled up and took him out of the stable and waited for the three cowboys. Soon the three came out of the hotel and walked to the livery. They saddled their horses, loaded their gear and the four men rode toward the Sterling Ranch.

The sun was going down but the weather was still warm. Jake thought a good rain could make it easier to trail recently rustled cattle but the sky was clear with very little chance of rain.

The ride was uneventful, but darkness had set in before they reached the ranch. When the four men rode into the yard they noticed a light in the window of the ranch house. Jake told the others to take the horses in the barn and meet him at the kitchen door.

Rachael had coffee on, and Jim Sterling was slaving over the tally sheets.

"Howdy, Jake," mumbled Sterling.

"Evening, Jim," replied Jake.

Rachael brought a fresh cup of coffee for Jake and warmed up Jim's cup. "I heard horses ride up," she said. "Do you have company?"

"Actually, I do, and they should be coming to the door at any moment," he replied. "I hope that you don't mind company."

"Depends upon who you brought," answered Jim.

"Dad, you know that we welcome anyone, or almost anyone, to our house. Shame on you," Rachael admonished her father.

Jake interrupted, "I think that you'll be glad to see these cowboys, and they can help out around the ranch." Just then there was a knock on the kitchen door.

Rachael said, "I'll get it," as she hurried to the door and opened it.

"Why, my goodness," she stammered, "good to see you boys again." She opened the door wider to allow the three cowboys to enter. "It's been a long time since any of you have been here," she added.

"Evening, Miss Sterling," said Rusty. The other two men nodded as they walked in the door.

"What brings you all to the ranch?" asked Rachael.

"Well, to tell the truth, we have been sitting on the fence between the Burke Ranch and everyone else just hoping that we didn't have to choose sides," replied

Rusty. "Something at the saloon today helped make up our minds."

"Howdy, Boys," said Jim Sterling. "Glad you came." The three men took off their hats, nodded to Rachael and spoke politely to Mr. Sterling.

"Jim, these boys have agreed to stay around the ranch for a spell and maybe help find some of your lost cattle," offered Jake.

"I know all of you boys, you're good cowhands and I appreciate your help, but you have to know that working for me is dangerous and could get you killed," said Jim.

"Well, Mr. Sterling, I got myself in some trouble in town today and Mr. Harn was kind enough to bail me out, so I think I owe him something," replied Rusty.

Billy added, "We were all in trouble, probably, if Mr. Harn hadn't come in when he did."

"What happened?" asked Rachael with concern in her voice.

"This gunman, named Jack Slade, came in the saloon and was trying to bully the three of us, telling us to move to another table. Rusty was going to shoot it out with him," explained Billy.

"You mean Jack Slade from Dodge City?" exclaimed Jim Sterling.

"The same," replied Jake.

"How did you know that it was Slade?" asked Rachael.

"I met Slade in Dodge City where he was working and witnessed one of his killings," explained Jake.

"Working, what type of work does he do?" she asked.

Billy interrupted, "Slade is a hired killer."

"Why is he not in jail, if he's a killer?" asked Rachael.

"Most hired guns are not wanted by the law," explained Jake.

"And how is it that men can kill others and not be wanted by the law?" she asked incredulously.

Jake looked at her and said, "Because they provoke other men to draw first and claim self defense when they shoot. The law rarely questions self defense shootings."

"Well, who in the world brought him to Burkeville?" asked Rachael.

"My guess would be that he was hired by Jeff Burke." suggested Jim Sterling, "But it might be difficult to prove."

"I agree on both accounts," replied Jake.

"By the way, Jim, I spoke to Brad Jason and he has agreed to meet with the other small ranchers. We'll soon find out if we can expect any type of support."

Sterling replied, "That's the best news that I've heard lately."

"Dad, just don't get your hopes up," said Rachael.

"Missy, we have to accept any type of hope regardless of where it comes from and how weak or strong it appears to be," he answered.

"Well, Boys, I am sure that you'll find everything you need in the bunkhouse," said the rancher.

"Yep, and maybe we can even locate some of the missing cows in the morning," replied Jake.

The three men said goodnight and headed for the bunkhouse knowing that tomorrow would be a busy day at the Sterling Ranch. Jake stayed for a few minutes to talk to Jim and then walked out of the door. As he headed to the bunkhouse in the dark he could hear somewhere in the distance a coyote howling out its lonely sound. He looked beyond the small clump of trees that shaded the pond but didn't hear any other sounds.

Sixteen

After a long night of drinking in the saloon, Jack Slade checked in at the hotel for the night. The next morning he got up, had breakfast at the café, asked for directions to the Burke Ranch, then rode out of town in the direction of the Bar B Ranch.

Slade thought about last night and wondered if Jake Harn was really the man he was supposed to kill. If he was not the man, he decided to kill him anyway because of his attitude. Slade was not used to having any man stand up to him.

An hour later he forded a creek near the ranch and rode into the front yard. He dismounted, wrapped the reins over the hitch rail and climbed the steps to the porch. He knocked on the door and soon a elderly housekeeper opened the door.

"Can I help you, Sir?" asked the housekeeper.

"I'm here to see Jeff Burke," said Slade.

"He is in his office down the hall. May I tell him who is calling?" she asked.

"Never mind, I will tell him myself," and he brushed past her and opened the door to Burkes office.

"See here …," she hollered, but Slade had already closed the door to the office.

Startled, Burke had looked up as Slade opened the door and he asked, "Don't you knock when the door is closed?"

"I don't knock on doors. My name is Jack Slade. Let's get to the point, I understand that you have a job for me," he said.

Burke did not like Slade's manners, but if he could take care of the problem with Harn, he could overlook them.

"Sit down," said Burke, "and I will tell you about my proposition. I own the biggest ranch in the territory and the ranch is rapidly getting larger. Everything was going smoothly until an outsider came in, killed my son and started trouble with some of the smaller ranches. I believe that he is even working for a ranch that I am planning to take over," he explained.

"And just who is this guy that is causing all this trouble?" asked Slade without much interest.

"Calls himself Jake Harn," replied Burke.

A wide grin came over Slade's face, and he nodded to Burke.

"Must be you're familiar with Harn," said Burke.

"I met him in Dodge City some time back and I ran into him again yesterday in town," replied Slade.

"How did you happen to run into him in town?" asked Burke.

"I was about to kill a gent in the saloon when Harn stepped in," replied Slade.

"Slade, I don't want you run out of town before the job is finished," said Burke.

"Burke, no one runs me out of town. Let's talk about the money," replied Slade.

Burke started to explain how he wanted the job done but Slade interrupted him. "Burke, I take care of the details, including the time and location, and you simply provide the cash," said Slade.

"Okay," said Burke, "two hundred fifty dollars now and seven hundred and fifty dollars more after the job is finished."

"I get half up front and the rest after the job is finished," replied Slade.

"How do I know that you can do the job?" asked Burke. "I understand from the boys that Harn is pretty good with a gun."

"He may be good but I'm better, and you'll just have to trust me," answered Slade.

Burke looked at Slade for a moment and said, "I'll give you the money up front, but I expect results, and I don't want a trail that can lead back to the Bar B."

When Slade didn't reply, Burke opened the safe, took out a cash box and counted out the five hundred dollars. He handed the money to Slade.

Slade counted the money, and Burke asked, "You don't trust me?"

"Burke, I don't trust anyone."

Burke stared at Slade and started to speak but

changed his mind.

As Slade walked out the door he glanced back at Burke and said, "I'll be back for the rest of the money after I kill Harn, and anyone else that gets in my way."

"Slade, be careful."

Slade strode out of the office putting the money into his pocket but at the front door bumped into young Matt Burke coming in. He glared at Burke and said, "Watch where you're walking."

Matt Burke looked at Slade and replied, "Keep your eyes open, and you can see."

"Who the hell are you?" snarled Slade.

"I'm Matt Burke, who are you?" he asked.

He immediately matched the name to Jeff Burke and decided to drop the issue. "None of your damn business," he said as he walked toward his horse.

Matt Burke turned and walked into the house and knocked on his father's open office door.

Jeff Burke said, "Come on in, Son, and have a seat."

Matt took a chair close to the desk and asked his father, "Who was the man leaving out of the house counting all the money?"

"Don't worry about it, Son, he's just someone that I'm doing some business with."

"What kind of business could you have with this guy?"

"I said, don't worry, I'll take care of it."

"Pa, why are we doing business with his type?"

"I just happened to need a job done that this man specializes in," replied Burke.

"This man almost drew on me after he bumped into me on the porch steps and you think we need him? He looks and acts like a gunman," he said.

"If you must know, he is a gunman, and he is the best. Once he's finished we will be in the clear and we'll have a free hand in the territory," explained Burke.

"Pa, why do we need more land? We have more than we're ever going to be able to use," replied Matt.

"Why you ungrateful whelp, I'm building all of this for you boys and you don't even appreciate it," he shouted.

"Pa, you are not concerned about Clay and me, and you never were. You built this ranch for Sonny and he left the ranch because of you."

Burke reached out and back-handed Matt who fell on the floor on his side. Burke looked at his son and said, "Sonny was a good boy. He had a wild streak in him, but he would've run this ranch the way I want it run. If you don't like my way you can leave."

Matt stood up holding his jaw and looked at Burke, "You're just not willing to admit that Sonny was no good. You can hit me all you want but that isn't going to change the facts," he said.

"If you're against me then move out," Burke shouted. Matt Burke looked long at his father and then walked out of the room.

Matt Burke was mad at his father and not just about the lick that he took from him. In his estimation things had gone from bad to worse when his mother died. His father was heartbroken, and to make matters worse, about the same time Sonny, the favorite son, began creating problems that his father had to fix.

Matt was sure that his father was trying to groom Sonny to take over the ranch, but Sonny was much too wild to stay in one place for any period of time. Matt believed after the shooting at Jones Crossing that his father knew that Sonny was not the man he was looking for, but he couldn't bring himself to admit it.

Matt gathered a few things from his room and started out the door. He stopped, turned and walked to the far corner, knelt down and with his pocket knife pried up the floor board closest to the wall. He carefully took out a small box, placed it in his shirt pocket, made sure the board was back in place, gathered his belongings and went to the barn. He saddled his horse, the one that he had trained from a colt, and rode into town. He went directly to the hotel and found Sarah Garnett. When they were alone he proceeded to tell her about the fight that he had with his father and said he was not going back to the Burke Ranch.

She put her arms around him and said, "Matt, why don't you stay here in the hotel until everything blows over. You can stay in room seven, next to mine."

"Sarah, I don't think that it's going to blow over. I'm

sure that my father hired Jack Slade to kill Jake Harn and, if so, I'm afraid that he has gone too far. It's inevitable that the federal marshals will be called in."

"Then we'll get married and leave town," she said.

"But what will we do for money and what will you do with the hotel?" he asked.

"I think that Mr. Stratton will keep an eye on it until I can sell it," she replied.

"Sarah, I love you, but I can't afford to make a home for you."

"Matt, the hotel is worth over twenty-five hundred dollars and I have a little money saved. We can make it," she pleaded.

"I do have a few horses that I can sell," he replied.

"Good, it's settled, I'll go over to the General Store and talk to Mr. Stratton. We also have a new young preacher in town named Joseph Foote. I am sure that he will perform the ceremony."

"Reverend Foote, I have not heard of him."

"I only met him once but I understand that he is from somewhere in Georgia,"

"If you think he is okay, he's okay with me. Dinner at the café later?" he asked.

"Love to," she said. "About seven?"

Matt handed the box that he took out of his room to Sarah and said, "How about keeping this for me."

She looked at him with a quizzical expression, and he said, "I'll tell you about it later."

Sarah smiled at him, placed the box in her pocket and walked out of the door. Matt watched her walk away, turned on his heel and headed upstairs to room seven.

Seventeen

As Sarah Garnett was working in the hotel she thought about the conversation with Matt Burke and his run-in with his father. Things had not always been so bad. Sarah was a couple of years older than Matt but she had had a crush on him for as long as she could remember. At first he was too young and did not pay any attention to her. Both Sonny and Clay Burke had tried to court her, but she was not really interested in either of them. Besides, her dearly departed mother would have whipped her if she had even looked at any of the Burkes. Her mother, Maggie, had known the Burkes for a long time even before Jeff Burke's wife, Trudy, died. The two women got along very well, and Maggie Garnett had spent many hours at the Burke Ranch but this was before Trudy Burke's death.

Things at the ranch changed drastically after her death. Jeff Burke became a bitter old man searching only for power and money. Most of his original ranch hands either quit or were fired and were replaced by gun hands. She wasn't sure if Roddy, the foreman, stayed out of his undying loyalty to the Burkes or the higher wages that Burke paid. He was not really a gun hand but he had been with the ranch for many years before Trudy's death and he had the knack of controlling the new men. Jeff Burke could always count on Roddy and that crazy man Fallon to keep the gunmen in line.

Once the gunmen were in place Burke began terrorizing all of the other ranchers. First he tried to buy them out and the ones that refused had their buildings burned, crops destroyed and ranch hands threatened. Initially, the ranchers fought to keep their land but the number of gunman on the Burke Ranch continued to grow. The ranchers became scared, and after some unexplained deaths, most sold out to Burke for whatever they could get and left the county. Many townspeople blamed Sheriff Ben Mason, but no one would back him against Burke's gunmen.

Things got worse as Sonny Burke grew up without his mother. He was wild as a child, but his mother kept him in check until her death. After that he was constantly in trouble and his father had to bail him out. She remembered the killing in Jones Crossing when everyone thought that Sonny would hang.

Matt was different from any of the others. He was handsome, kind and gentle. Unfortunately, his disposition got him in trouble over and over with his father. Matt wanted to live in peace, and he knew that many people hated him and his brothers because they were Jeff Burke's sons. The difference was that the other two didn't care whether they were liked or not. Clay was the oldest, and even though he was much like his father, he got less attention than Sonny.

Sarah remembered the day that she decided that she was going to marry Matt Burke. It was the day her mother died and Matt came to the cemetery. Afterwards they took a walk and talked and talked. Matt did not mind that she cried after every other word. He was not courting her, he was just being a friend when she really needed one.

He continued stopping by the hotel when he came in town to see how she was doing, and they became closer and started talking about marriage. Neither of them had much money. She had inherited the hotel but not much else. Matt was getting paid from his father but he was sure that if he married Sarah his father would cut off the money. Sarah didn't care. She was sure that they could live in the hotel and that Matt could get a job.

And then there came Jake Harn. Sarah had not met anyone like Jake. He was extremely handsome and was either the bravest or the dumbest man she had ever seen. When she tried to talk to him he just smiled and laughed it off. She hated to admit it but her heart fluttered every time he was around but she couldn't . . . .

Her thoughts were interrupted by the desk clerk. When she got downstairs she found out that it was almost seven and she had agreed to meet Matt for dinner.

She talked to the desk clerk for a few moments, got her wrap and headed to the café. Matt Burke was sitting at a corner table, and she headed directly toward him. He saw her coming and stood up and waited for her to arrive.

"Sorry I am late," she said. "I had some things to do."

"I'm just glad that you came," he replied.

Johnny stopped at the table and exchanged pleasantries until the two of them ordered and she hurried off to the kitchen. When they were alone, Matt said, "I've been thinking, and I believe that we should get married quickly."

Sarah was delighted and could hardly control her emotions. "I'm so happy, I've dreamed about this moment for a long time, but..." Her voice trailed off.

'What's bothering you?" asked Matt.

"What about your father?"

"Sarah, I've decided that I loved my father once but I'll never be able to live with him again. That means that it's time for me to move on with my life and my life is with you. There may be some problems, but I'm willing to face them if you're with me."

"Oh Matt, you know that I'll be with you."

"Then let's not wait. We can be married on Saturday."

"But Matt I have so much to do to get ready for the wedding."

Matt smiled at her and asked, "Do you think that you can be ready or do you think we should postpone it?"

"Oh, no," she smiled, "I'll be ready."

Johnny came along with the food and said, "You two seem happier than I ever remember. What's going on?"

"Johnny, we're getting married this Saturday."

"Why congratulations, I'm happy for you, but..."

Sarah interrupted her, "I know the "but," and we're going to face everything together."

"Well, enjoy your dinner but we've got a lot of planning to do," said Johnny.

"I hoped that you'd say that," Sarah replied, "and I want to invite everyone in town."

"Everyone?" asked Johnny, "How about Jake Harn?"

Sarah's face turned red and she tingled at the mention of his name. "Yes, we'll even invite him—if he's still alive."

Eighteen

Jake and the new riders from Sterling Ranch ate an early breakfast and rode out to locate and round up as many cattle as they could find. After several hours of hard riding, they had only located a few hundred cows. According to Jim Sterling, the last count should have been close to five thousand head of cattle and only about twenty-five hundred could now be accounted for. Jake left the other three men and decided to scout closer to the Bar B Ranch.

He had been riding through underbrush and valleys when he stopped to water Muddy and get a drink of water for himself. He took the rifle from its boot and carried it with him. He then loosened the cinch from the saddle and allowed the horse to drink his fill. Jake moved a few feet up stream, took off his hat, laid down his rifle and lay down on his belly. He drank from the stream and then splashed water on his face to get rid of the trail dust. He took several long drinks and just as he raised his head, a rifle shot sounded and the bullet kicked up dirt and sprayed water a couple of feet from where he was lying.

Jake grabbed his hat and rifle and scooted a few feet to the left where he had more cover. He leveled a round in the chamber, aimed at the area where he thought the shot came from and pulled the trigger. Two more shots were fired, all close to where Jake was located. He aimed again and got off two more shots hitting into the vicinity of the ambusher. He waited for a few moments and hearing no more shots he sprinted to where Muddy was cropping grass. He took the reins and led him behind an outcropping of rocks a few yards away. He tied Muddy and took out his field glasses and scanned the ridge several yards away. He lay there for several minutes, but saw nothing and heard nothing more from the ambusher. He aimed the rifle, pumped a couple more shots toward the area where he thought the ambush was coming from and got lucky. He saw a glint of the rifle barrel and then saw a flash from the ambusher. The shot was wide but Jake poured several shots in the area and thought that he heard someone yell. He waited a few minutes and he heard a horse riding off into the distance.

It appeared that there was only one gunman, but Jake was not going to take any chances. He carefully raised his head to look around. After a few minutes he walked toward his horse, being careful to stay down low enough to make a smaller target just in case there was more than one bushwhacker. He led Muddy as he worked his way around the ridge so that he could get a clear view of the location from where the shot came from. When he got where he thought was the best view, he lay down on his belly, listened and waited. Nothing happened. Jake decided to get a closer look. When he reached the spot, no one was there but there were horse tracks and spent rifle cartridges. From the tracks Jake decided that there had only been one horse. He picked up the shells and examined them. They were from a Spencer Rifle. He put the shells in his pockets and moved a few steps to where the horse tracks were. He soon noticed that the tracks were the same as the ones he found at the Sterling Ranch and at the hidden meadow.

Jake wanted to visit Old Jed at the livery stable before going back to the ranch, and it was getting late. He mounted and headed for town.

When he saw the lights of town, he circled and came in from the east near the livery stable. As he dismounted he decided that since the sun was going down he would stay in town rather than ride back to the ranch. Besides, he thought, he may be able to get a glimpse of Sarah in the hotel. Old Jed came out of the barn and greeted Jake. Jake gave him instructions and handed over the reins to the old man. He turned to go but then decided to ask Old Jed now about the tracks that he found near the ambush site. At this point he decided not to tell him about the attempted ambush. He described the tracks in detail and Old Jed said, "Yep, I do know 'bout them tracks, they belong to Dave Egan's horse, he works for the Burke Ranch."

"How long has this Egan feller been around?" asked Jake.

"Nigh on six months I reckon," replied Old Jed.

"Do you know anything about him?"

"Not other than he came along with several other gun hands hired by Burke."

Jake nodded to Old Jed and replied, "Thanks."

"Mr. Harn, can I ask, what's your interest in Dave Egan?"

Jake thought for a moment and then told the story about the tracks in the meadow and the same tracks where the attempted ambush took place. He then asked Old Jed to keep his inquiry secret, at least for now. Old Jed nodded.

"Thanks again," said Jake, and he headed in the direction of the café.

Nineteen

Jake walked to the café and ate his fill of Johnny's stew and bread. Johnny assured him that he could get a steak, but he politely refused and stayed with the stew. Afterward, he relaxed for several minutes while drinking coffee. He then left the café, checked on Muddy at the livery stable and headed for the saloon. As he walked in he noticed that business was slow, with only two men sitting at a table drinking beer. They were both strangers to Jake. He ordered a beer, drank it quickly, and headed toward the Burkeville Hotel. His mind was clearly on Sarah, the proprietress of the hotel. He thought that he could even sense the faint smell of the perfume she wore. He then decided he was a fool for even thinking about her. The few times he had spoken to her she had not been warm and friendly. In fact she was downright hostile. Even so, he couldn't stop thinking about her.

Jake walked to the hotel and asked for the key to room seven but the desk clerk told him that room was occupied. He accepted another room, turned to go upstairs and noticed Sarah Garnett in deep conversation with a young man. A second look told Jake that it was young Matt Burke.

Disappointed that he would not be able to get a chance to talk to her, he went up to his room. He checked the door but it didn't squeak so he moved the water stand in front of it. No sense taking chances, and any noise would alert him in time to react. He had trouble sleeping because of all of the things that were going through his head. Finally, he dozed off but woke early. He decided to get up, have breakfast, and head on out to the ranch.

He dressed, left the hotel, and had breakfast at the café. Johnny was talkative and Jake thought about asking her why Sarah Garnet disliked him but decided not to.

He finished breakfast, saddled Muddy, and rode out of town. Jake was not in a hurry so he gave Muddy his head. He was mulling over the events of the past few days and was trying to come up with some answers. None came to mind, so he thought about Sarah Garnett and Rachael Sterling. He got no answers there, either.

He had been riding for some time when he sensed that he was being followed. He let Muddy slip into an easy lope and tried to hear what was going on but nothing came to his ears. Jake was wary and couldn't shake the idea that someone was staying right with him, but out of sight. When he rode into a clump of trees he decided to see if he could flush out whoever it was. He stopped the horse, draped his reins over a small limb and pulled out the Henry from the rifle boot. He walked quietly to the opening of the brush and waited for something to happen. He waited. He wanted a cigarette, but he knew that the smell from the smoke could be detected from far away, so he discarded that notion.

Several minutes later he heard the unmistakable sound of a walking horse. He stayed low to the ground and undercover until the horse and rider passed about twenty feet from where Jake was crouched.

"Hold up, Mister, and don't turn around."

The rider started to turn but Jake shouted, "If you turn around—you die."

The rider had an idea who he was facing but he decided to wait for a better time to find out. "Okay, Mister, don't shoot."

"Just unbuckle your gun belt and let it drop," ordered Jake. The rider did so without hesitation. "Now step down and stay where I can see you." The rider obeyed, walked in front of his horse and got his first glimpse of Jake Harn up close. He hoped that he could talk his way out of this because he knew Harn's exploits with a gun.

"I have no money, Mister," he said, "but I'll give you whatever I have."

"I don't want your money and I think you already know that. What I want is to know why you were following me," Jake replied.

"You're making a mistake, Mister, I wasn't following you."

"Step away from your horse," ordered Jake.

The man did as he was told and Jake walked up to the horse. He kept his eye on the stranger and picked up the right hind leg of the horse. The shoe was loose and the print of the warped shoe that Jake was looking for fit this horse. "Dave Egan, I presume," said Jake.

"How do you know my name?" he asked.

"Your horse told me," replied Jake.

Egan thought about that comment for a moment and then said, "Okay, now that you know who I am, what are you going to do?"

"First of all, tell me why you are following me and why you took pot shots at me," stated Jake.

"I didn't …"

"Skip the lies, Egan," interrupted Jake. "You were looking for me at the Sterling Ranch when your friend drew on me. Also, I've been following your tracks for several days after I saw you and your friend holding the cattle in the ravine."

"Mister, I don't know what the hell you are talking about. I don't know nothin' 'bout no cows and I've never seen you other than at the Sterling Ranch," he said, raising his voice.

"You are involved in rustling cattle because I was there and I identified you and your horse with the cattle. No need to deny it," replied Jake.

Egan blurted out, "Taking the cattle was not my idea, it was Bur...," his voiced trailed off.

"Was it also Burke's idea to ambush me?" asked Jake.

"I'm not saying any more," replied Egan.

"Well, let me fill you in. You and your friends could not kill me, so Burke hired Jack Slade. You still wanted to get the money so you wanted to get me before Slade got a chance. How am I doing so far?" asked Jake.

"I don't know no one named Slade," replied Egan.

"You don't have to say anymore, I'll do the talking." Jake took out a piece of paper and pencil and gave it to Egan. "I want you to write what you have already told me and you can get out of the territory safe and sound."

"I won't do it, Burke will kill me."

"Burke won't have to kill you because I'll kill you first. Start writing quickly or I'll kill you now," Jake pointed the gun barrel right at the belt buckle of Egan.

"You son of a..."

Jake interrupted and said, "I'm losing patience with you. You can write or drag iron." He stooped, keeping an eye on Egan, picked up the gun and holster, and tossed them at the feet of Dave Egan. "Put it on or write."

Egan stared at the gun and holster and remembered Diego drawing on Harn. Finally, he decided to write.

When he got finished he handed the note to Jake.

Jake read it and pushed it in his shirt pocket. He walked up to Egan's horse, tied the reins on its neck and swatted the horse on the hind end causing it to gallop off down the trail.

"What are you doing? You said that I can leave," yelled Egan.

"That's right, Egan, you can leave and make sure that I do not see you in this county again."

"But, the nearest town is ten miles," Egan flared.

"I make it closer to twelve." Jake picked up the gun belt and hooked it on his saddle horn. "I will drop this off down the trail and I don't expect to see you again."

"Damn you Harn, I'll..."

"Get started," said Jake, "before I change my mind." Egan started trudging down the trail cursing Jake to high heaven. Jake stepped in the saddle and rode off toward the Sterling Ranch.

Twenty

Jack Slade would do anything for money and he would go to any lengths to protect his reputation as a ruthless gunman. Part of his plan was to bully his victims so that they would get so angry that they would be forced to defend themselves, but he was not sure that he could antagonize or bully Jake Harn. When he had looked into those cold blue eyes he decided that he might have to find another way to get Harn angry and frustrated.

Today he believed that he found the answer. Harn had taken up residence at the Sterling Ranch and apparently become attached to someone there. The rumor was that that someone might be the beautiful daughter of the owner of the Sterling Ranch. Slade thought about kidnapping her but he decided that even if Harn were tied to her it would not be a good idea to harm her. The code of the west was very strict about harming women and Jack Slade did not want a rope around his neck.

His second idea was to deal with someone that was close to her and assume that Harn would be loyal enough to intervene. After thinking about it for a while Slade came up with the perfect person.

Jim Sterling and the hands had spent several hours rounding up strays without much success. He decided to take Sam and move south to a water hole that normally kept the attention of many of the cows. Rusty, Steve and Billy were left to finish the search.

He and Sam rode along for awhile and Sam spoke. "Jim, I think someone is following us."

"Sam, I think you're spooked. Why would anyone want to follow us?" asked Jim.

"I don't know, but I am rarely wrong about this. I thought I saw someone earlier on, but I wasn't sure. Now I feel it in my bones," he replied.

"Sam, your old bones could probably feel anything that they wanted to. Well, we'll stop at the water hole, allow the horses a drink, look around and head back to the ranch," said Jim.

"Not too soon for me, I'm worn out," answered Sam.

"And your old bones," Sterling joked.

"Don't laugh, you'll be old some time if you live long enough."

A few minutes later the two men arrived at the water hole and dismounted. They allowed the horses to drink and stooped down to drink for themselves.

Just as they were finished a voice came from behind them.

"Stand up slowly and turn around." The two men stood and turned to see a stranger holding a gun pointed toward them.

"Who the hell are you?" asked Jim Sterling.

"Jack Slade. Does the name mean anything to you?"

"I've heard of you, Slade. What do you want?"

"I have what I want: you, Jim Sterling."

"Well, now that you found me, speak up, I'm busy," replied Sterling.

"Well I guess that there's no harm in telling you, I'm looking for Jake Harn."

"Harn is not here, and I've not seen him for several hours. Harn works for me so what do you want him for?" asked Sterling.

"I plan to kill him," Slade smiled and pointed the gun at Sterling, "and you are going to help me."

"Go to hell, Slade, I won't do anything for you," Jim replied.

"I think you will if you want to keep your daughter safe," retorted Slade.

"You touch my daughter and I swear to God that I'll kill you," replied Sterling with his anger quickly building.

"How about now, Sterling, you got a gun?" sneered Slade. Slade dropped his gun into his holster and added, "We're all even."

"You'd love for me to go for my gun so that you could claim self defense."

"Well, you don't have to, but I'm sure going to enjoy meeting your daughter face to face."

Sterling hesitated and Sam said, "Don't do it, Jim."

"I've not seen her, but I've heard that she is quite a looker. You can imagine what I am going to do with her." he retorted. "I might even just take her with me when I leave."

"Why you…," Jim's voice trailed off as he went for his gun.

Slade was much faster and he shot Sterling twice. The first bullet hit him in the right shoulder and the second hit him in the right leg near the thigh.

The rancher went down with his gun still half in his holster. He was writhing in pain when Slade spoke, "You'll live, and I want you to take a message to Jake Harn. Tell him I'll be waiting for him in town to kill him."

"Go to hell, Slade, I …" his voiced trailed off.

Sam knelt down by the rancher and Slade looked at the two men and said, "Don't forget to deliver the message." He walked back to his horse, mounted and headed toward town.

Sam was not a doctor but he had seen many gun-shot wounds and he believed Jim Sterling was in bad shape and would get worse unless he could stop the bleeding. While he was bent over, he heard horses and he pulled his gun and turned around.

"Sam, you don't need that gun," replied Rusty. "We

heard shots and came running."

"What happened to Mr. Sterling?" asked Billy.

"Jack Slade shot him," said Sam.

"Why the hell would Slade want to kill Jim Sterling?" asked Billy.

"He didn't want to kill Jim. He just wanted to get at Jake Harn. After he shot Jim he told him to tell Jake Harn that he would be waiting for him in town."

"How is he?" asked Steve.

"He's in bad shape. He's lost a lot of blood and moving him may cause him to bleed more," replied Sam.

Rusty answered, "We have to get him back to the ranch so let's get him bandaged and get going."

"Steve, you ride hard to the ranch and get a wagon and some blankets."

"But Rusty, that's an hour to get there and back," protested Steve.

"Can't be helped, we'll fix him up best we can and we'll take him back to the ranch in the wagon when you get back. Now git going."

Steve had his doubts but he kept them to himself and rode off toward the ranch at a gallop. Rusty looked at the other cowboy, "Billy, high-tail it to town and fetch Doc Gray, tell him to meet us at the Sterling Ranch, pronto."

"I'm on my way," replied Billy, and he leapt on his horse and galloped off toward town.

Sam and Rusty finally got the bleeding stopped

best they could. All they could do now was keep Jim comfortable and wait for the wagon to arrive.

⚜

As Jake was getting near Burkeville he heard a rider heading his way at breakneck speed. He pulled off the trail so that he could get a look at the horse and rider. The rider was not trying to hide his identity so Jake was not concerned for his safety but he was curious as to who would be riding at that speed.

When the rider got closer Jake recognized him. It was Billy Cannon, one of the riders from the Sterling Ranch. Jake nudged his horse and moved into the path of the horseman and raised his hand to stop him.

"Whoa, Pardner," said Jake, "what's the blame hurry? You're going to kill that horse."

"Jake, Jim Sterling has been shot and I'm going to fetch the Doc and take him to the ranch," a breathless Billy replied.

"How'd it happen?" Jake asked.

"Jack Slade shot him and told him to tell you that he would be waiting in town for you."

"Go ahead and get the Doc. I'll meet you at the ranch," instructed Jake. He wheeled Muddy and headed for the ranch at a gallop.

After an hour or so, Jake finally rode into the ranch. Sam was sitting on the steps with his head in his hands. He looked up at Jake and said, "Jake, I told him not to draw on Slade but Slade just kept egging him on with threats about Rachael."

"That's how Slade works. Forget about it Sam, you couldn't have stopped him. Slade is a master at provoking men to draw, and then he claims self-defense," replied Jake.

"How is Jim?" Jake asked.

"I don't know. We had to bring him in on a wagon over rough terrain, and he has lost a lot of blood. I don't think he is even conscious now."

Jake turned and went inside the house. Jim Sterling was lying on the bed with Rachael and Rusty at his side. The shoulder had been bandaged, and Rachael was trying to stop the blood that continued to bleed from his hip.

Rusty turned to Jake and said, "Glad to see you, Jake."

Jake nodded to Rusty and spoke to Rachael. "How is he?"

"I don't know," came her anguished reply. "He's not been conscious since they brought him in some time ago."

Jake looked at Jim and then Rachael. "He'll be okay. I saw Billy, and he and the Doc should be here very soon," said Jake.

"Jake I don't know what I'll do if my father dies," she began to sob gently.

Jake put his arm around her to comfort her, and

Rusty decided to take his leave. "I got work to do. I'll see you two later," he nodded to Rachael and Jake and walked out of the room.

Some time later Jake and Sam were drinking coffee and Rachael was pacing around the room waiting for Doc Gray to finish patching up her father.

"What's taking so long?" asked Rachael. "He's been in there at least an hour."

"Be patient, it's a good sign that he's still in there," Jake tried to encourage her but she was not persuaded.

At that moment the door to the bedroom opened and Doc Gray came out looking grim. The three looked at him for answers, but he just stood there. After a few moments he said to Rachael, "He'll live and his shoulder will be fine but the hip is more serious."

"What does that mean?" asked Rachael.

"Well, it could mean he'll never ride a horse again," he answered.

"It'll break his heart, but I'd rather have him alive and not be able to ride than dead," Rachael replied.

"Now Rachael, you know your father. He'll try to get out of bed, but you've got to keep him lying down. Someone needs to be with him all the time and make sure that he doesn't put any pressure on his hip until I come back," said Doc Gray.

"How soon will that be?" she asked.

"Couple of days. I can't do anything right now anyway, but send for me if anything changes." He looked at Jake and said, "Jake, I'd love to have some of that coffee if you've not drunk it all."

"Oh, sure. Doc, I was so worried about Jim that I forgot my manners," replied Jake.

"You roughnecks don't have any manners, do you?" asked Doc Gray.

"Now, Doc, Jake is a southern gentleman. I'm sure that he has some of what you call manners," replied Sam.

Jake tried to ignore the banter as he poured a cup of coffee for the doctor. Doc Gray took a couple of sips from the coffee and looked at Jake seriously. "How are you and all of your wounds?"

"Don't worry, Doc, I'm healthy as a horse."

Doc Gray looked at him doubtfully and said, "And you wouldn't tell me anything else anyway, would you?"

"I'll come and see you if I need to, Doc."

Doc Gray finished the coffee and gave the cup back to Jake, "Well, got to go. See you in a couple days." He waved and went out the door.

Sam escorted him to his buggy. "Thanks for your help."

"Sam, you just help Rachael keep that old goat in bed. You know how ornery he is. Moving around too much might do more serious damage."

"We'll take good care of him, Doc."

Doc Gray turned the buggy and drove out of the yard, heading toward town.

Later, Jake walked out on the porch and sat down with Sam. "Jake, what are you going to do about Jack Slade?" asked Sam.

"Well, I'm going to pay a visit to him in town. That's what he wants," replied Jake. "Where are Rusty and the boys?"

"They rode out a while ago to check on cattle, but I can get them if you want them to back you up," answered Sam.

"I'm going into town by myself and I don't want you to say anything about me leaving. If they knew they might want to interfere and someone could get killed. I'll be back later on, so ask the boys to stay close to the ranch."

"Jake, someone might get killed and it just might be you. Just what do you hope to accomplish by going into town alone?" asked Sam.

"Sam, this is something that I have to do, and I need for you to be quiet about it to the boys, and especially to Rachael," replied Jake.

"Don't like it a bit, Harn," warned Sam.

"There's no other way, so just do as I ask."

"Will do," said Sam with his eyes showing genuine fear.

Jake nodded to Sam and strode to the barn. He saddled his horse and headed for town.

Twenty-One

Jake knew that the shooting of Jim Sterling had nothing to do with the rancher. It was a challenge to him and because of the challenge Jack Slade would not attempt to ambush him. Slade was a cold-blooded killer, but he had his pride and he wanted everyone to know when he killed a man. His plan had always been to provoke his intended victim, attract a large crowd so they could see his victim draw first. Then he killed. He wanted to make sure that the law always knew that he did not draw first. He had stayed out of jail by always having plenty of witnesses.

Keeping this information in the back of his mind, Jake decided that it was safe for him to ride into town in plain sight. He was counting on the fact that Slade would be in the saloon and that he would be drinking. Slade had a bad habit of drinking too much when he waited. Jake decided he would give Slade enough time to drink as much as he wanted before facing him.

Jake casually rode into town and wrapped Muddy's reins around the hitching rail in front of the saloon. He had no concerns about Slade but he was aware that other men from the Burke outfit might want to help collect the bounty by ambushing him before he met with Slade. His eyes roamed the immediate vicinity, but did not see anyone lurking near the saloon. A few people were on the street, but they were unaware of the shooting that was to come. Jake decided that the only people that knew would be those in the saloon.

Jake climbed the steps, walked in and hesitated just inside. The first thing he saw was Slade standing at the bar with a glass of whiskey in his hand. Jake guessed that he had been drinking for some time. This could be the advantage that Harn needed when Slade went for his gun. He looked around the room and noted six other men drinking. Four of them were playing poker at the corner table; the other two were sitting at a table in the corner drinking.

Slade looked at Jake and snarled, "I guess that you have some backbone after all. I thought that you would have been several miles away from here after what happened," he added.

"I'm sorry to disappoint you, Slade."

"Harn, I'm not disappointed, I really expected you to come."

"Why the shooting of Jim Sterling? I would have come without it," replied Jake.

"Insurance," answered Slade.

"You knew that Sterling was not a gunfighter," said Harn.

"Harn, he had a gun just like everyone else that I've shot, and I even spared Sterling's life," retorted Slade.

"You should be grateful."

"Of course you knew Sterling, like everyone else that you've shot and killed, could not match your skill with a gun," said Jake.

Slade countered, "No one can match me with a gun, and you're going to find that out soon enough."

"That's the reason I'm here, to find out," replied Jake.

"You're going to be sorry about that," responded Slade. He drank down the rest of his whiskey and slammed his glass down on the bar.

"Slade, I'm getting tired of your loud mouth. If you're going to make a move, go right on," replied Jake.

Slade was surprised by the aggressive tone of Harn's words. Most of his victims were scared. Harn was not scared, but it wouldn't matter in the end, thought Slade.

"Slade, have you gone soft?"

Now he was getting angry. He stepped away from the bar just as the bartender pulled out a shotgun from the bar and spoke loudly, "There will be no gun play in my establishment. If you want to kill each other, take it outside."

Slade turned and glared at the bartender and said, "Stay out of this."

The bartender pointed the shotgun directly at Slade and said, "I can't miss at this range, Slade."

"You just signed your death warrant, Friend," said Slade as he headed out the door.

Jake stepped out of the way and waited for Slade to walk past him. After a moment, he followed him out. Jake looked around and noticed that Sheriff Mason was heading toward the saloon. He decided that the best thing to do was to keep the sheriff out of the fight.

"Jake, you want me to intervene?" the sheriff asked.

"No thanks, Sheriff, you might just get yourself killed. Just keep your eyes peeled for any of Burke's gunmen," replied Jake.

"Harn, I don't need any help and, Sheriff, you just bought your ticket to Boot Hill, too," said Slade.

Jake noticed that a crowd was beginning to form, and he wanted to get this over with.

"Slade, you talk too much. There are a lot of people here waiting. You don't want to bore them to death with your loud mouth do you?" asked Jake.

"You're a dead man," said Slade as he reached for his gun.

Two shots were fired almost at the same time. Fortunately, Jake leaned to his right and the shot grazed his left shoulder. Jake's bullet caught Slade in the chest. He stared at Jake and his knees began to buckle, "You shot me, you son-of-a-b...," said Slade as blood gurgled from the bullet hole in his chest. Slade tried to lift the gun again to shoot at Jake but he lost his balance and collapsed in the dust of the street.

Jake carefully walked to Slade and kicked the gun out of his reach. Slade was pretty far gone, but he still tried to speak. His face was full of hate and he stammered, "Harn, you're not getting out of here alive. If Burke's men don't get you, brother Buck wi ... wil ... kill...." He took his last breath and died.

The sheriff walked over where Slade's body lay.

Jake looked toward the sheriff and spoke, "In case you've not heard, Slade shot Jim Sterling earlier today. He provoked him to draw by making crude remarks about Rachael. Sam witnessed the whole thing. Doc Gray says that Jim will be down for some time."

"Sorry to hear that. Hope he will be okay and I'll try and visit him tomorrow," replied the sheriff. "Some of you boys get this body to the morgue," he added.

"Harn, I would suggest that you get that arm fixed, there's a lot of blood," said the bartender.

"I didn't know Slade had a brother. Do you know anything about him?"

"Only by reputation. He has a gang of cutthroats that raids in and out of Kansas and hides out in the Indian Nations. There's no doubt that he will find out about his brother's death. I'm just not sure how close they were," replied the bartender.

"I'm not familiar with the Indian Nations that you're talking about."

"A large part of the Oklahoma territory has been assigned to Indian tribes and there's no law in those areas," explained the bartender. "Outlaws raid into Kansas and Arkansas and hide in the area. "You don't need to worry about him right now. Get along and have Doc check you out."

"I guess I should before I start back to the ranch," Jake said. "And, by the way, Sheriff, how about meeting me at the café in about a half hour?"

"Glad to," he said. "It'll be close to dinner by then anyway."

Jake went to Doc Gray's office and, before he could explain, Doc said, "Making a habit of getting shot, aren't you, Harn? The other wound hasn't even healed up all the way."

Jake explained what happened in the street and about his wound. Doc Gray looked at it and said, "You're lucky. The bullet went clear through and it appears to be a clean wound but you've lost a lot of blood. Again."

He examined the wound, cleaned and bandaged it and gave Jake a sling for his arm. "You may want to rest that arm for a couple of days and stay away from my office for a while," suggested Doc Gray with a smile.

"Sorry, Doc, I have some unfinished business with Burke. I am going back to the Sterling Ranch as soon as I have a chat with the sheriff, but I will try to avoid your office," he added. Jake paid the bill and turned to go.

"Be careful. If the wound starts bleeding you could

be in trouble," replied the Doc.

"I'll be very careful. By the way Doc, how is Jim Sterling, really?" asked Jake.

"He'll be okay, but he's going to be in bed for some time and will not be able to ride for several weeks. I cautioned Rachael to keep him in bed, but he's a cantankerous old fool, and I'm sure that he won't follow my orders," answered Doc.

"Much obliged, Doc," said Jake as he walked out of the office and headed for the café.

When Jake walked into the café, the sheriff was already seated, drinking coffee. He greeted Jake, "I was beginning to think that I was going to have to buy my own dinner."

"I can't imagine an upstanding lawman having to buy his own dinner," quipped Jake.

"You'd be surprised," shot back the sheriff.

The two men ordered food and chit-chatted until the food came and they spent the next few minutes enjoying the stew and bread. After Johnny came and cleared the dishes she brought more coffee and Jake began to speak. "Sheriff, a few days ago, you offered me a deputy badge. Is that offer still open?"

"Harn, what do you have up your sleeve?" asked Ben Mason.

"I want to arrest Jeff Burke and take him to Hays City for trial," answered Jake with a coldness that the sheriff had never seen from him. The sheriff's first impulse was to laugh but the seriousness in Jake's manner stopped him cold.

"Harn, I realize that you are good with a gun and that you killed Jack Slade, but I'd like to remind you again that Burke has plenty of men still at the Bar B and most of them are gunmen."

"Sheriff, I'm not going to take on the whole group, I just want Burke. I believe that if I get him, the rest of the gunmen will scatter in different directions," replied Jake.

"How are you going to get Burke without his henchman, and besides, what makes you think that you can make any charges stick?"

Jake took out the letters from Judge Ben Robichaux and Dave Egan, "I believe with these letters I can make it stick."

The sheriff read both of the letters and asked Jake, "How in the world were you able to get the letter from the judge and the confession from Egan?"

"Let's just say that the judge had a change of heart. Egan was a little more difficult to convince," said Jake.

The sheriff handed the letters back to Jake. "That appears to be enough evidence but you're still going to have to get Burke out of the county."

"Sheriff, I spoke to Brad Jason and he agreed to try and help."

"How can Jason help with his small number of men?" asked the sheriff with some doubt in his voice.

"He's agreed to try and persuade some of the smaller ranchers to get their hands together and ride to where the stolen cattle are being held."

"You trying to get those men killed?"

"No, Sheriff, I just want them to get close enough to draw fire from Burke's men and then skedaddle before the shooting begins."

"Well, it might work, but they will need to be very careful," replied the sheriff.

"Brad Jason is an ex-army officer and I'm counting on him to create a diversion and get out before anyone gets hurt," explained Jake.

"Sheriff, can you get onto the ranch and speak to Old Man Burke without getting shot?" asked Jake.

"Well, I think I can, but how is that going to help you?"

"Sheriff, I have a plan, and if you're willing, I think we can pull this off," said Jake. He outlined the plan in detail, and, despite some reservations, the sheriff agreed to cooperate. "Now wait for the signal from Jason before you go in," warned Jake.

After they finished their coffee, Jake paid the tab, and the two left the café. Jake's horse was still tied in front of the saloon and the two men walked over there. They had only taken a few steps when Jake saw the huge shadow of a big man at the door of the saloon. It had to be Fallon, he thought. At the same time the sheriff saw what he was looking at and said, "What now, Harn?"

"Sheriff, I don't have the time or the energy to take on Fallon again, if he causes problems I'm going to blow his head off."

"I think that we can persuade him to behave."

As the two men approached the big man, he stepped in front of them to block the sidewalk. Jake slipped the colt from its holster as the sheriff spoke, "Fallon, I'd suggest that you get back into the saloon."

Fallon looked at the sheriff and then stared at the colt in Harn's fist. Reluctantly he turned away and walked back into the saloon.

Jake slid the colt back into the holster and wiped his brow with his shirt sleeve. "I don't want to tangle with him again."

The sheriff grinned and said, "Harn, you're smarter than I gave you credit for when I first met you."

"Well, Sheriff, some times your first instincts are wrong," smiled Jake.

"Could be, let's get you deputized," said the sheriff as he turned and headed for his office.

Jake watched the sheriff walk away and thought, it's possible that I was wrong about you too. He walked to Muddy, untied the reins and followed the sheriff to the jail. After the sheriff swore him in, Jake put the badge in his pocket, walked outside for a smoke, then mounted and headed to the Sterling Ranch. He thought over the plan again in his mind as he rode. He had some concerns, as did the sheriff, but he did not want the sheriff to doubt the success of the plan. He was still mulling over the plan when he rode into the Sterling Ranch yard and dismounted at the barn. He heard the kitchen door open and he recognized the distinctive features of Rachael Sterling. She was hurrying toward Jake. When she got close she had tears in her eyes and she said, "Jake, I was really worried about you, I was afraid that you would be killed and with Dad crippled what would I..."

Jake took her in his one good arm and kissed her gently, "Everything is going to be fine," he assured her. She clung to him for several minutes with the tears streaming down her cheeks. After a few minutes she composed herself and stepped away from Jake.

"I know that I'm a fool and I know that you can take care of yourself, but I just . . ." her voice trailed off.

Then she noticed the fresh bandage. "You're going to get yourself killed!"

Jake replied, "I know that you have some coffee in the kitchen and maybe some apple pie," he suggested.

She knew that he was avoiding her comments so she smiled and said teasingly, "Don't you ever think about anything except food?"

"As I recall, I've not been offered anything better," he chuckled.

Twenty-Two

The next morning Jake woke up very early, dressed, and stopped by Jim Sterling's room. He appeared to be resting comfortably, so he mounted Muddy and rode out. He was careful not to wake Rachael because he didn't want her to know where he was going or what he had planned.

Jake's plan was to have the sheriff visit the Bar B Ranch and talk to Jeff Burke. He would tell Burke that they found the cattle and needed help driving the cattle back to the ranches and ask him if his men could help. The aim was to get as many Bar B riders as possible to leave the ranch. He would explain that he had no idea who was responsible for the rustling. Certainly, when Burke found out, he would try to move the cattle. If his plan worked, it would not be difficult to later round up the cattle and divide them among their owners.

Then the plan was for Jake to get Burke off the ranch and transport him to Hayes City before his gunmen could return and interfere. His arrival at the ranch would have to be coordinated with the sheriff's news of the stolen cattle. He circled the ranch and found a slope that would allow him to watch the house but not be seen. He tied Muddy to a clump of brush and waited. The arrival of the sheriff would signal that everything was a go.

He hoped it would not be long, but he was used to playing a waiting game. He built a smoke, took a few puffs and waited. For some strange reason he thought about Quincy Cranbrook. The little man was like a bandy rooster and he was obnoxious, but for some reason Jake had taken a liking to him and he certainly appreciated the warning in the telegram.

His thoughts went from Quincy to Rachael Sterling and the goose bumps he had felt when she touched him while tenderly changing his bandages. And he saw the concern for him in her beautiful face and her sweet smile when he kidded her. She was a truly remarkable woman.

Jake was still thinking about her an hour or so later when Muddy raised his head, snorted and looked off to the distance. Jake cleared his mind, took his field glasses and identified the sheriff as he was heading for the ranch.

It probably would take a while, so he found a vantage point where he could keep tabs on the sheriff and the ranch. He took a swallow of water from his canteen and rolled another cigarette.

Some time later Sheriff Ben Mason rode into the Bar B Ranch yard, dismounted and spoke to one of the hands. A few minutes later Jeff Burke and what Jake assumed was Clay Burke came out of the house. The conversation was brief but animated. The old man was shouting but Jake could not hear what he was saying. A bit later, the sheriff mounted his horse and rode off in the direction of town.

Jake knew that it would not be long now. If his hunch was correct the bunkhouse would be emptied and most of the hands would be riding out. Only a few moments passed before Clay Burke and the foreman came out the door and strode toward the barn hollering instructions as they went. Clay Burke did most of the hollering. It only took a few minutes for everyone to get saddled up and ride out of the yard.

Jake had no idea exactly how many men Burke employed so he would just have to take his chances with anyone that stayed behind. He decided to leave Muddy in the clump of trees and move toward the house on foot. He crept forward using as much cover as he could find and he kept as quiet as possible. From an early conversation with the sheriff, Jake believed that Burke would have at least three people in the house, other than himself. The first two would be the cook and the housekeeper. They were both elderly so the sheriff did not believe that either of those two would provide much opposition. But the sheriff had told Jake that Burke always kept one of his gunmen in the house when the other riders left the ranch. This could be a sign that Burke did not use a gun, and if so, Jake would be happy about that.

Jake reached the ranch house undetected and hugged the wall until he found the door that he thought was the kitchen. He took the deputy's badge from his vest pocket and pinned it on his chest. He then turned the door knob and it opened. Jake slipped in with his revolver in his hand and his eyes scanned the room. Jake gently closed the door behind him. The wide-eyed cook turned to face him. He immediately raised his hands and said, "Don't shoot, Mister."

Jake pointed to the badge pinned on his chest and said, "You won't be harmed if you stay calm and do as you are told."

"Yes, Sir, Deputy," he choked out the words.

"Now just walk to the far corner and don't move until I come back," he warned the cook.

The cook moved to the corner, covered his eyes and nodded agreement.

Jake walked out of the kitchen into the dining room. The room was empty but he noticed that across the room was another door that Jake believed had to lead to the living room. He walked to the door and put his ear to the door and listened. There was a conversation in the room and one of the voices was female. Jake figured that had to be the housekeeper but the other voice could be Burke or the guard.

He went back to the kitchen and spoke to the cook, still cowering in the corner, "Go into the dining room and call for the housekeeper."

"What for?" he asked with a trembling voice.

"I want you to call her into the dining room and be very careful about how you do it," ordered Jake.

"But, Mister, she don't spend much time in the dining room. She will know something's wrong when I call her."

"We'll just have to take a chance. Do it, and do it quick," ordered Jake as he leveled the gun at the cook's chest.

The cook slowly walked into the dinning room and complied with the request to call for the housekeeper. She came through the door and said, "What do you…" her voice trailed off as she saw Jake holding a gun on the cook. "What's going on?" she stammered.

The cook looked at her and said, "Be quiet. He has a gun."

Jake looked at her and said, "I am a deputy sheriff from Burkeville, and all that I want you to do is stay in the kitchen and be quiet."

The cook said, "We'll do it. Just don't shoot us."

The housekeeper was bolder than the cook. "I didn't know Sheriff Mason had a deputy."

"It was a sudden appointment," explained Jake.

Jake looked at the two, the cook cringed and backed away while the housekeeper glared at Jake.

"Lady, I heard voices in the room before you came in. Who was the other voice?" asked Jake.

"I don't know what you're talking about," replied

the housekeeper.

"I'm a patient man, but I have just about reached the end of my string. You tell me what I want to know or you will be locked up with Burke," demanded Jake.

She hesitated for a moment but decided to cooperate. "His name is Ray. I don't know his last name. He always stays in the house when the men ride out."

"He carries a gun?" asked Jake.

She hesitated a moment, "Yes."

Jake motioned them to the kitchen then walked to the living room door. He slipped it open slowly trying to find the location of the man named Ray. He didn't immediately see the man but he did see smoke curling above a chair with its back to the door. His luck was holding so far.

He pushed the door open a little farther and slipped into the room. The man with the cigarette stood up and turned around to say something to the housekeeper but he froze when he saw Jake with a 45 pointed at him. "Who the hell are you?"

Jake interrupted, "Deputy Sheriff. Just keep quiet, unbuckle your gun belt, and let it fall."

"I'll be damned if I . . . ."

"You'll die if you don't, do it quick."

He started to protest again but Jake stopped him again. "Now," he said, and stared at the man with his cold, deadly eyes.

The man hesitated but then did as he was told and

asked, "Now what?"

"Mister, I have no quarrel with you. As long as you do as I tell you, you're okay," replied Jake.

"Burke pays me to protect him."

"You have muffed that job, so you may as well get on your horse and ride out."

"I won't do it. Burke or his men will kill me for sure."

"You will quietly walk out of the door, get your horse and get out of the territory. And if I see you again I'll kill you before Burke's men get a chance," answered Jake.

"But I have money coming," he protested.

"If you die you'll not have any use for money," replied Jake.

"You bastard," he murmured as he turned and stalked out of the house.

Their voices had not been loud, so it was possible that Burke had not heard any of the conversation from the living room. He edged toward the office door and listened for any sound inside the office. He heard nothing. He tried the door and it opened. Jake pushed it open a little wider. Burke was sitting at his desk, and had not heard Jake slip into the room.

"Stand up, Burke, with empty hands. You are under arrest," said Jake.

Burke, startled by the intrusion, looked up and said, "Harn, what the hell are you doing here?"

"I am taking you to Hayes City for trial," replied Jake.

Burke tried to compose himself and said, "By what authority do you plan to arrest me?"

"Deputy Sheriff of Burkeville, Kansas, duly sworn in by Sheriff Ben Mason," said Jake.

"Harn, if I call out you're going to be a dead man."

"That bluff isn't going to work. I took your man's gun and sent him down the road," replied Jake. "Also, your hired gun, Jack Slade is at the undertaker's office as we speak."

"Now you are bluffing," said Burke. "There's no way you killed Jack Slade."

"Well, if you need verification about Slade you'll have to visit the morgue. If you think that I'm bluffing about your guard, just call out."

Burke hollered out but nothing happened. He called again with the same results. "I told your cook and housekeeper to stay in the kitchen and your henchman has already moved on. Now just do as you are told," said Jake with an icy tone in his voice. Burke looked at the desk, and Jake said, "If you're reaching for a gun in the drawer, it will be your last move."

"Harn, you have no evidence against me that will hold up in court, and I'm a rich man. Let's just see if we can make a deal," he said.

"No deal, Burke, and all I need for evidence is these two letters," he said as he pulled out the letters from his shirt pocket. One is from the judge in Jones Crossing and the other is from one of your gunmen named Dave Egan."

"Harn, I don't know either of those people."

"We'll just have to let the judge in Hays City make that decision, won't we?" replied Jake.

He hollered again for his henchman and suddenly reached for a 38 revolver in his desk. Just as the gun came above the top of the desk, Jake shot him twice. The first bullet hit his right shoulder and the second hit him high in the chest. Burke staggered and looked wide-eyed at Jake and said, "You, you…," his voice trailed off as he slumped to the floor.

Jake closed in and kicked the gun away from Burke's hand, but it was not necessary, Burke was dead.

The cook and the housekeeper rushed into the room and stared at the body of Jeff Burke.

"Your boss is dead, I want you to go for the sheriff and you may also want to get the undertaker," said Jake.

The cook looked at Jake and then Burke and said, "I'll go," and hurried out of the room.

"Mister, what I am I going to do now?" asked the housekeeper.

"I am sorry, Ma'am, but I'm sure that you will be okay."

Just then Jake heard the sounds of horses and men yelling. From the sounds it would be the Bar B riders coming back. He suspected that they would be in a bad mood. He sure wished that he had brought his shotgun, but it was too late for that. He looked at the housekeeper and asked, "Is there a shotgun in the house?"

"On the wall, up the stairs," she replied.

"Thanks," he said and dashed up the stairs. He had no time to waste. He found the shotgun. Luckily, it was loaded because he had no idea where to look for shells. He came down at the same time the riders rode into the yard. Before they had time to dismount, Jake walked out the front door with the shotgun.

"What the hell are you doing here?"

"Who's asking?" replied Jake.

"I'm Clay Burke and ..."

Jake interrupted, "Guessed that you would be Clay. Your guard and Dave Egan have both skedaddled from the territory. Jack Slade and your father are dead."

Clay looked at Jake and said, "Who killed my father?"

"I did, he went for a gun in the desk drawer, and I shot him. Now there is no reason to continue to keep these gunmen on your payroll," replied Jake.

"What right did you have to kill Mr. Burke?" asked Roddy, the foreman.

"Deputy Sheriff of Burkeville," said Jake as he pointed to the badge pinned on his chest.

"And just who the hell had the nerve to deputize you?" asked Clay.

"Mr. Burke, you and your hired guns are no longer in charge of Burkeville. The sheriff is rounding up all of your men that are not here and putting them in jail." replied Jake.

One of the riders on Burkes left spoke up, "Well, that's not good enough for me," he said as he reached for the hogleg on his hip.

Jake wheeled toward the man and fired a barrel from the shotgun. The blast knocked him off his horse and caused him to scream in pain. Jake ignored the man and turned the shotgun back to the crowd. "I have one more barrel and I can take several of you with me. Now my suggestion is that you collect any wages you have comin' and get out of the county," said Jake.

"Pay 'em off, Clay, it's not worth it. You may be able to salvage something if you don't get killed," suggested the foreman.

Clay stepped down and walked into the house. A few minutes later he came back with a bag of money. The money was distributed, and all of the men rode out except Clay and the foreman. The other riders had to help the wounded man on his horse. He was still moaning in pain.

Jake unloaded the shotgun and handed it to Clay Burke. Burke looked at Jake and said, "Harn, this isn't over yet."

"I hope so for your sake and mine because, I for one, am tired of shooting and killing," replied Jake.

Twenty-Three

Just as Jake was heading back to get his horse, the sheriff, Rusty and several townsmen, including the bartender and Lattimore Q. Cranbrook, rode in. And to Jake's surprise Rachael Sterling was with them. She dismounted and ran into Jake's arms.

"I was so worried when the sheriff told me what you were planning to do," she exclaimed.

"The sheriff talks too much."

"Don't blame him. I forced him to tell me," said Rachael.

"Harn, she is very persuasive. By the way, I hear that your prisoner got himself killed," said the sheriff.

Jake looked at the sheriff with a quizzical expression and asked, "How did you hear about that?"

"First of all we met the cook riding as if he was being followed by the devil himself and then we met the remainder of the Bar B gunmen heading south. One of them mentioned that Burke was dead and that they were heading out," replied the sheriff.

Jake looked at Rusty and asked, "Did the cattle get rounded up?"

"Yeah, Boss, we've moved most of them and Brad Jason and the other ranchers are finishing up. They are checking the brands and moving them to the right ranches," explained Rusty.

"Good news," said Rachael, "it looks like most of the cattle from the Sterling Ranch will be returned. By the way, Mr. Harn, I have kept a secret from you because of my own selfishness," she continued.

"A secret? I didn't think you could keep a secret," said Jake as he put his hand on her arm.

"Mr. Harn, do you remember the young woman that you raved about in your sleep that first night?" asked Rachael.

"Miss Sterling, I have no idea what you are talking about," replied Jake.

"When we first brought you to the ranch, you were out of your head and talked about several things while I was tending you."

Rachael looked very sincere and Jake had the sinking feeling that he was caught in a trap. "Okay, just let me have it."

She was enjoying this now and so were the men waiting for her to finish the story.

"Well, you were talking long and loud about her. I was sure that you would remember her for some time after you woke up," she kidded.

"I don't remember talking in my sleep, and I still don't know what you're talking about," said Jake.

"Sarah Garnett, that's what I am talking about."

The others gathered around, laughing at Jake's discomfort but he was not conceding anything. "What about her?" asked the surprised Jake Harn.

"According to your own words, she is the most beautiful women in the world," replied Rachael.

"I, I uh …"

Rachael interrupted him with a smile and said, "Well, she's getting married on Saturday,"

The sheriff chuckled and said to Jake, "I understand that you even got an invitation. By the way, that young man over there is Reverend Joseph Foote and he is going to do the marrying. Reverend, this is Jake Harn."

"Hello, Reverend," said Jake.

"Would you be Major Jake Harn?"

"Yes, I used to be. Do you know me?"

"Actually, my brother Sergeant Grover Foote served in your unit. He talked a lot about you."

"I remember Grover very well. He was a good soldier." Jake looked closely at the reverend. "I don't remember seeing many men of the cloth wearing a gun."

"Sometimes God needs us to help our ownselves and living in this country is one of those times."

"Reverend, I can't argue with that."

Jake looked back at Rachael with a twinkle in his eye and said, "You, young lady are very funny. By the way, who's she marrying?"

The bartender interrupted Jake and said, "You remember the conversation that you and I had about the lady at the hotel and Matt Burke?"

"Yep, I remember," answered Jake.

"Well, Sarah Garnett is marrying Matt Burke," said the bartender.

"I think that's good news," said Jake with as much enthusiasm as he could muster. "By the way, Sheriff, how does this play out with the Burkes and the Bar B Ranch?" asked Jake.

"I spoke with young Matt and Miss Garnett and I am convinced that Matt had nothing to do with the shootings and killings that surrounded the Burke Ranch. I also spoke to the judge, and he agrees with me," said Sheriff Mason.

"And Clay?"

There probably is not enough evidence to try him, so he will most likely go free if everything can be worked out," replied the sheriff.

"Forget about all of this. We're going to have a big wedding celebration, why, I suspect that just about everyone in the territory will be there," suggested the bartender.

"This territory has finally had something to cheer about and I suspect that it'll be long and loud," said Rusty.

The sheriff smiled at Rachael, turned to Jake and said, "I have to admit that I was skeptical when you came into town, but you made a believer of me and most of the town folks."

"Sheriff, I appreciate the help that you provided. If

it wasn't for you, it would have been very difficult to get the evidence on Burke," Jake replied.

"Maybe we can team up again," said the sheriff, "if you are planning to stay around town for a while."

Rachael answered the question before Jake could respond, "The competition has been eliminated, and if I have anything to say about it, he'll be here for a long time."

"You heard that, Sheriff, and I rarely disagree with a beautiful woman," said Jake jokingly.

The sheriff gave Jake a knowing grin, mounted his horse, tipped his hat to Rachael, "I expect to see you and Rachael at the celebration," he said as turned to ride toward town.

Rusty spoke to Jake, "I'll get the boys on back to the ranch and finish the tallying. Come on, Boys."

"Thanks, Rusty, I'll be along after a while."

Just that moment Quincy sidled up to Jake. No matter how hard he tried, Jake could not dislike the little man. He looked at him and said, "Hello, Quincy, good to see you again and thank you for the telegram."

"No thanks needed, Jake, but I do have some news also."

Jake looked at Quincy and said, "Well, spill it. I hope that it's not about writing a book about me."

Quincy ignored the sarcasm and said with a smile, "I'm getting married, too, and settling down in Burkeville."

Jake looked at Quincy with astonishment. "You're getting married! Anyone I know?" asked Jake.

"I don't think so, I met this wonderful widow in Dodge City, and she was working at a newspaper. We decided to start a newspaper in Burkeville, and I'll be able to write my articles."

Jake was skeptical but wished Cranbrook luck.

"By the way," Quincy continued, "I'm not giving up my job with Colt Manufacturing. I have become a partner in the gun shop with Mr. Johnson. I can still sell my merchandise."

Jake put his hand on the colt 45 and smiled at the little man. "I'll be around to see you, but we are never writing a book about me."

The little man smiled back at Jake and replied, "Never is a long time, Mr. Harn, and dime novels are making lots of money back east." He climbed on his donkey and headed for town.

Rachael turned to Jake, looked up at him and said, "Jake, I know that you were riding on when you got here but I would really like for you to stay here on the Sterling Ranch. With Dad crippled the way he is, we are going to need a lot of help," she added.

"I know," said Jake smiling and looking at Rachael. "There is a lot of work to be done and you are short-handed. I have a strong back and a weak mind, and you want to take advantage of me."

"Look, you big-headed fool, you are not that good

as a cowboy so you may need to sell yourself some other way," she said as she turned toward her horse.

Jake took hold of her arm and turned her toward him. "Maybe I can think of some other way to impress you if you'll give me a chance," said Jake.

She smiled a little and put her hand on his arm, possessively. "Come. I am sure that I can think of something if I try hard enough."

He started to speak, but she shook her head. "Wait till we get to the ranch and we'll have a long talk."

Jake picked up the reins of Rachael's horse and the two walked without speaking back to the thicket where Jake had left Muddy. He helped Rachael on her horse, untied Muddy and put the reins over his neck. Jake started to mount but instead turned back to Rachael, "I certainly hope that we can do more than just talk!"

She smiled a devilish smile, looked at Jake and said in a soft voice, "Silly boy."

LaVergne, TN USA
06 December 2010
207531LV00001B/56/P